THE FAMILY THAT *Stays Together*

Half Dozen Publications

Author's Note:

This is a work of fiction. The events described are imaginary and the characters are fictitious. It is not intended that any reader infer that the events or settings are real or that they actually happened. Resemblances to actual persons, living or dead, or business establishments are products of the author's imagination and used fictitiously.

ISBN: 061577363X
ISBN-13: 9780615773636
Library of Congress Control Number: 2013933926
Half Dozen Publications, Westborough, MA

To the Women Religious

Who Witness to the Complexity of Life's Challenges and

Make Our World a Better Place

CHAPTER 1

I didn't expect Jessica to turn the interview on *Good Morning, Atlanta* into a therapy session, but she did just that. As a seasoned journalist having won several local Emmys early in her career as a news anchor in Cleveland and even more awards since she moved to Atlanta ten years ago, she had the ability to personalize questions and get the support she needed for herself while still managing to make the content just as personal for her viewers.

"So, Dr. Carpenter, the part of your book that I found really intriguing was the chapter on truth-telling. I have been on both ends of the dilemma of whether or not to tell. I actually bumped into a friend's spouse at a club with another woman…" She gave a long sigh and tossed her head from side to side, the soft, shoulder-length, blonde-streaked mahogany curls in rhythm, mimicking the black soul-sister-girl expression. "… and I have had a friend tell *me* that they saw my man stepping out on me." She gave a deeper sigh and directly faced the camera with a look that asked viewers to join her in disbelief that this could have possibly happened to her.

Jessica's easy style and vulnerability endeared her to a loyal, large audience and kept the ratings for her award-winning urban news magazine program at the top of the charts. She was everyone's girlfriend, sister, and confidant. She bumbled so charmingly through her days that you could not help but just shake your head, sigh, and walk through life hugging her. The producers loved how she tended to over-share on camera. This was obviously one of her times for over-sharing.

As a result, I tossed the scripted questions from my PR firm onto the side table along with my prepared responses and hoped that the camera being projected to the viewing audience was not on me. I knew better than to glance over to the monitor. No matter how many times I had done television appearances, my startled reaction would give me away. The startle response of seeing yourself on screen let the viewing audience know that you were a little freaked out by your face staring back at you. I had done enough television interviews to know that if you weren't sure of what to say, you just waited for a question and avoided babbling. Knowing Jessica's interviewing skills, babbling would definitely be dangerous. Thank God, after about a second, Jessica quickly asked a question.

"Dr. Carpenter, should you tell your friend if you know that her partner is cheating?" She paused. "Or I suppose it could be his partner as well? Women do cheat on men, and for gays and lesbians, same gender, same problems, as they say." She patted note cards on her knee. I knew that question was not on those cards.

I began talking slowly while the forming sentences came across my mind as if on ticker tape. "The role a friend plays in a faltering relationship due to cheating is a popular chapter in the book." I smiled, struggling to focus the conversation on the theories posed in the book rather than discuss on air a personal feud between Jessica and my sister on whether her ex-fiancé had cheated on her.

"Whether you should tell or not depends on a number of factors. First, whether or not you have actual facts about the indiscretion or are you just going on hunches, perceptions, or a feeling." I paused, shrugging my shoulders while smiling at Jessica. "Second, it depends on the strength of the relationship that you have with your friend."

"Well, in my case, the friend that I knew whose husband was cheating, I did actually see him in, let's just say, an intimate encounter with a woman that I knew for sure was not his wife. So, I had facts. That was your first point." She paused and smiled back at me. "On the second point, although I have known her for many years, we were really more like acquaintances, and I suspect she would not be happy with me getting in her business, especially business she might not know about." She turned toward the camera, convincing the audience that her assessment was right. Turning back to me, she sought my confirmation. "So, I guess you would recommend not saying anything to her."

I gave a gentle laugh. "Well, it sounds like the strength of that acquaintance would probably not withstand such a disclosure. It would be very awkward, and I suspect the friend would question your agenda for providing her with that information."

"Okay, that makes sense. Now, in the case where someone told me, the person is like a sister to me. We are very close. So, you would say that it warranted telling me?" Oh God, please tell me she didn't just go there. Here I was, in front of millions of viewers with Jessica fronting on my sister Tina. Straining my face to avoid a look that was sure to be interpreted by the viewers as, "Oh, no you didn't!" I prayed the camera was not positioned on my face and that I could keep focused. I quickly pretended that I was talking to a head of lettuce.

"Well, the other condition would be the veracity of the information. Was it rumor, suspicion, a hunch, or direct contact like the encounter you had with your friend?" Oh, poop! So much for moving the conversation away from personal. Jessica beamed.

"Hmmm ... that's a good question. My friend would say it was factual, and I would say she made an assumption that the woman was not just a good friend. We went back and forth over this for months, like junior high school girls." Jessica chuckled.

I joined her imagining the scene with Tina and Jessica ready to pull out each other's clip-on hair pieces. "It really boils down to trust, doesn't it? How much do you trust your friend and your partner? Only you would know if your friend is offering solid support, or if your partner is telling the truth about the nature of his relationship." As I spoke, Jessica shifted herself in the studio chair hanging on to my words as if discovering the answer would save her life. Her reaction served as a reminder that this was not a therapy session although it was really feeling like one. Did I see tears welling up in her large brown eyes or was I imagining them? I moved forward in my chair; my psychologist reflex was working to assure her that things were okay.

"Ultimately, it is not about how much you trust your friend or even your partner. It's about how much do you trust *yourself*." Jessica sat back in her chair with such a pensive look on her face that it made me think that, despite all her years in front of those cameras, she might have forgotten that we were on air. "There's a lot more of that discussion in the book," I said a little too loudly with an excitement that stemmed more from anxiety than a shameless pitch to sell books. Jessica was definitely having a long aha moment. To the relief of both of us, the producer twirled a finger in a circle, signaling to Jessica it was time to wrap the interview. Like Pavlov's dog, she was conditioned to react quickly to the gesture and instantly went back into TV anchor mode.

"And information about where you can obtain this best-selling book is on your screen. My thanks today to Dr. Kathy Carpenter, psychologist and author extraordinaire, for a most enlightening discussion." She nodded, smiled, and patted my knee while reading from the prompter. "We can keep the conversation going by visiting our Facebook page or joining us on Twitter. That information is also on your screen, along with the information on Dr. Carpenter's new book." She paused and winked into the camera, adlibbing, "This is a topic I know we will be buzzing about for a while." Back to the prompter. "Thanks for joining me. We will talk again tomorrow. Good Morning, Atlanta, and make it a great day!" Sound technicians rushed to the platform, removing the microphones from Jessica's white Chanel wool tweed jacket and removed the one off my vintage navy blue blazer.

"Great interview, Kath! Thanks for letting me get this exclusive." Jessica guided me through the spacious studio. The newsroom was larger and more modern than the local station in Cleveland where I was regularly featured as a guest psychologist offering commentary on everyday local issues to breaking world news of the day. The narrow pathway was lined with low cubicles, and Jessica scurried through them like a well-trained mouse in a maze. I worked to keep up with her swift pace, and in lieu of stopping to engage staffers, I nodded and smiled back as they looked up from their computers acknowledging me as Jessica's celebrity guest.

The release of my latest book in the series of *You and Your Partner* had quadrupled my clinical practice and propelled my local celebrity status to what was now national exposure. It required being responsive to what my newly acquired PR firm called my fan base. It was all a bit surreal. Establishing a relationship with a "fan base" was so different than building rapport with a willing patient. That relationship could easily be achieved in three one-hour sessions and did not have the distraction of cameras or microphones. Outside of the limelight of television interviews, even as a best-selling author, I privately hoped that I would remain unrecognizable to the public. That was one good thing about the interview with Jessica. Curiosity was sure to be raised about her cheating partner rather than remembering me as an author.

"I really do think this is the best of the books in the series. And it's such a hot topic with all that is going on in Congress," Jessica continued. *You and Your Partner... When Mental Illness Separates,* written five years ago, had given birth to a whole series of *You and Your Partner* books ... *When Religion Separates ... When Income Separates ... When Addiction Separates.* The rapid rise to a national bestseller of the latest book, *When Cheating Separates,* was probably more indicative of a larger target audience than the other books in the series. After all, the divorce rate in the United States hovered slightly above 50 percent. Still, I remained surprised that the simple advice I had given to Cleveland couples when a partner had cheated translated into a *New York Times* bestseller.

The advice that resonated most with readers was actually very simple. It took two days to complete. On the first day, you lived as if your partner was completely out of your life, perhaps thinking about him or her being buried under a jail for whatever hurt and pain he or she may have caused you.

On day two, you were to experience the day as if all were forgiven and you now shared a happy home with your partner. At the end of each day, you recorded how you felt and then compared the journal entry from each day assessing which day brought you the most peace and resolve. Surprisingly, stories describing readers' two-day experiences were sent to the publisher in record numbers. I could write another book just with the happy home and under-the-jail stories. Go figure.

"Or maybe I think it's the best one because the topic is so close to home," Jessica paused as if to consider her ranking of the series or maybe to think through her earlier aha moment. She then quickly abandoned either thought, dismissing the energy it would take to calculate her ranking of the book or to go deeper on an insight. Instead, she shrugged her shoulders and then waved her right hand in a forward movement gesturing me to follow her into her corner office. Entering, she quickly picked up a stack of newspapers on a chair and nodded for me to take a seat.

"It will only take a minute for me to wrap things up, and then we can leave to meet Tina for dinner."

"No problem. I've got time. I'm not heading back to Cleveland until tomorrow." I paused, surveying Jessica's office. "There weren't any decent flight times that I could make without killing myself to get there, so I just booked a flight for the morning. Besides, it gives me an evening to spend with you and Tina."

I leaned back into the cushioned chair that was

surprisingly comfortable for office furniture and was now positioned in the line of sight of the five Emmys, numerous plaques for community service, and framed photographs of Jessica with celebrities like Lady Antebellum, Raven-Symone, Kelley Rowland, Cee-Lo Green, Tyler Perry, Paula Dean, William Andrews, and Ryan Seacrest. Several photos of Jessica and Don Davenport, another Cleveland transport to Atlanta, to whom Jessica had recently been engaged, gave pause to my scanning. The breakup was no surprise to anyone, as Don and Jessica had been in and out of each other's lives since their high school days, returning to each other after college breakups and most recently after each divorced. Jessica followed my gaze landing on a picture of her and Don draped in leis, most likely from a Hawaiian vacation during more pleasant times. Her smile immediately dissolved as she noticed what had captured my attention.

"I'm sorry to hear that it's over for you and Don." I consoled her and almost added "again," but stopped myself. It was far more natural to extend comfort and support to Jessica; her innocence was exposed, and her genuine good nature was always open. At first, Don was a good match for her. He was fiercely protective, unfortunately to the point of jealousy. In the end, his street-wise personality outweighed Jessica's authenticity, and it became impossible to live in each other's world. If I took back the hours of listening to Tina release her frustration about Jessica's version of unconditional love, I would have a few days added to my calendar.

Then, two months ago, Jessica surprised us all and ended the relationship with little explanation of any precipitating cause. We were so happy that she was now focused on moving forward that no one probed for details.

"I know it's yucky to have everything be so public about your relationships, Jess. You don't get a chance to fall apart privately, do you?"

"You can say that again, which is why I hope you didn't mind if I got a little personal during the interview. There's been so much gossip about Don cheating on me as the reason that we broke up that I wanted to put it on the table that I wasn't completely blind to the possibility." Her voice trailed off to give pause to ponder their separation.

The interview had gotten hijacked with Jessica's emotional connection to the topic oozing out. It saddened me that Jessica felt obligated to explain her life choices to strangers.

"All set," Jessica said, interrupting my thoughts. "Let's get out of here before I get pulled back into some Atlanta mess that needs to be broadcasted."

The walk to the front lobby took only a few seconds. Leaning her right shoulder, she pushed the swing door forward to enter WBS TV 2 News' front lobby. Over Jessica's five-foot-five-inch frame, I was delighted to see my sister Tina. We quickly moved toward each other.

"Sister Nun, you did a great job bashing all those no good, low-down, lying, fucking cheaters in the interview." Tina grabbed me in her signature bear hug and tossed the top of my hair as if I were an adored little granddaughter. It was her signature big sis/little sis gesture, although in our behaviors, our ages always appeared reversed. I was forty-four years old and Tina was fifty years young, going on twenty-five. She still lovingly called me Sister Nun, my nick-name from my twelve years spent as a nun before I married Jon Hoffman, whom she affectionately called the White Guy.

"Tina, thanks. And watch your language." Tina laughed and I joined her. I couldn't help cringing hearing the F bomb and Tina knew it. The word never did get incorporated into my vocabulary, despite numerous attempts by Tina to spice up my language and achieve a greater impact when I expressed emotions. Hearing me say "doo doo balls" instead of simply saying shit annoyed her. We went many rounds of verbal tennis with her as my coach for how to curse like an adult. "Doo doo balls." "Shit." "Doo doo balls." "It's shit." "No, it's doo doo balls to me." Peals of laughter descending between us.

Tina even once tried to transfer my knowledge of behavioral therapy desensitization techniques to learn how to say fuck, drilling me with homemade flashcards.

"Can you say truck?"

"Can you say luck?"

"Can you say fuck?"

Nope. Never could.

I hugged Tina back hard, taking in the scent of fresh linen from her body spray. It had been only a month since I had seen her, and phone calls could never capture such an embrace.

"I thought we were meeting you at the restaurant? What a blast that you showed up here." I pulled back from Tina and examined her black leather thigh-high boots, textured hose, and maroon mini skirt. The houndstooth jacket and lace blouse were a surprise contrast with the mini skirt, but no surprise for Tina's playful spirit that always expressed itself in her distinctive fashion style.

"Tina, I had just told Kathy you were meeting us at the restaurant. I'm glad you caught us." Jessica smiled lovingly at Tina and gave her a hug. As an only child, Jessica had considered us her siblings from as far back as our childhood days.

"I wanted to actually get here for the interview instead of watching it on my iPad, but that crazy Big XL wouldn't approve the fabric I had chosen for the living room curtains. Why that fat pig with his country-ass taste needs to put his half-a-cent into my design plan is beyond me."

Tina made a lucrative living as an interior designer whose clients were primarily Atlanta rappers and hip hop artists. Her mission as a designer was to upgrade their taste from ghetto fabulous to suburban chic. She was usually successful with most of her clients, but obviously Big XL was proving to be an exception.

"Where are we going for dinner?" The question was directed to either Tina or Jessica as I suddenly experienced an intense onset of hunger that I hoped would also serve to quench Tina's desire to continue discussing firing her client.

"We aren't going out to eat." Tina did a quick dance

shuffle, throwing the straps of her bag over her shoulders so she was free to snap her fingers. "I made some kick-butt gumbo and corn bread. We're going back to my place where we can puts our feets up…take our hairs off…and throw back some wine." Laughing at her own coined phrases, Tina grabbed Jessica and me and marched us through the door.

Tina's design talent extended to cooking. With our stomachs full of the spicy mixture of shrimp, chorizo, crawfish tails, and Creole seasoning, we took full liberty spreading ourselves on Tina's overstuffed couches.

"Girl, you threw down that gumbo," Jessica sighed. "Don would have cleaned that pot. He loved your gumbo!" Jessica threw her shapely legs over the arm of the beige chaise lounge as she balanced her wine glass.

"Hmm…the way he treated you, Jess, I would make sure there was a little pesticide in his dish. I don't like cockroaches in my house." Tina was on her second glass of wine, but even without alcohol, she was known for being brutally honest.

"Don't be so hard on him. He's really a good man with a kind heart. It's my fault that you grew not to like him. I shared too much of his faults with you over the last months and not enough about the good. He was getting his life and finances together. He had been successful in his job for the last five years." Tina stuck out her tongue at Jessica who ignored her childish antics. "Yes, he hurt me, and I have moved on," she declared. "I'm just trying to hold on to the good memories and trying to learn the lessons God intended for me to learn from the time we had together."

"Now ain't that about a blimp, a bug, and a booger." In addition to childhood gestures of sticking out her tongue, Tina now included childhood language. "You are no way over that man, Jess. And the only lesson God intended for you to learn was, when any man can't handle his money and he has a wandering dick, you got to run—and not walk—as far away from him as you can. Me, myself, and I would cut that dick off for cheating on me before I would kick him to the curb, but that's me. The bottom line is, you move as far away from him as you can, even in your thoughts. Sister Nun Psychologist would agree, right?"

"I'm not touching this conversation, and I am especially not giving out any advice ... unless somebody's going to pay me." I quickly added.

"He didn't leave Jessica with any money to pay anyone." Tina turned directly to me and then turned back to Jess. "How could any man call himself a man and have you taking care of all his business? That ain't right."

"Tina, you forget that I *willingly* loaned him that money, and all the checks were not made out to him personally, so I have a record that some of his loans were paid by me. And despite us not being together anymore, he intends to pay me back every dime. He told me so just last week."

"And if you believe that, then Sister Nun here is a prostitute. I don't call someone clearing your bank account without your permission a loan just because it wasn't preapproved. And why are you still in contact with him, Jess? Come on now. If it's about the money, you know I can and will cover you until you can get back on your feet. Clean break, Jessica. Cold turkey. Drop him like he's hot. Hit the road, Jack. Run, Forest, Run." The red butterfly pillow Tina threw across the room landed on Jess's face just as Tina intended.

"I am. I am. Just be patient. It takes a while. I'm just grieving the loss of what could have been a great marriage. Right, Kathy?" Tossing the pillow on the floor, Jessica turned to me for support.

"That's so true, Jess." I comforted her, agreeing with the first part and choosing not to argue about what her imagined outcome would have been for a marriage to Don Davenport. Who of us had a crystal ball?

"Yeah, you believe Kathy, who had hopes of living happily ever after in Africa with Ibaaka Akwesei?" Tina and Jessica began laughing uncontrollably.

Newly sprung from the convent, my first serious relationship was with a black studies professor from Ghana, West Africa. When we broke up, I read a string of self-help books like *Why He Can't Commit* and *How to Break Your Addiction to a Man*, cried endlessly on Connie, my office manager's, shoulder and practically had to move in with my sister Dana who wanted to put me on suicide watch.

"That's not fair. I may have been older, but for all practical purposes, I was just picking up from high school. No different from when you broke up with your first love. Y'all know that." I pleaded with Tina and Jess for a little mercy.

"I got a lot of practice after Ibaaka and plenty of relationships that I didn't even shed a tear about." I was working hard to convince them, yet Tina and Jessica looked at me dubiously.

"It's true. There was the bus driver who didn't own a car but got us discount bus tickets for riding all over the city. That financial broker who tallied up every relationship-related expense and divided them evenly," I paused, recalling how food, movies, theater, video rentals, cost of gasoline, even overhead attributed to the wear and tear on sofas and dining room chairs were calculated. "He was really weird, and I didn't shed a tear over him." Tina and Jess were giggling like junior high school girls hearing about a round of an adolescent kissing game.

I paused, remembered, and spurted out. "Then there was the Buddhist white guy that I didn't even realize I was dating until he called me and told me that he didn't want to date me anymore. That one kept me laughing for days."

"But you fell apart big time again with Marlon." I was surprised that Tina remembered any of my relationships, especially when she had a string of them herself to keep up with. Tina had married her college sweetheart and then divorced him when her daughter Melody was a toddler. She remained close to her ex and dated numerous men—most of them were considerably younger. By dating significantly younger men, it allowed her to remain committed only to herself and her work. Lately, Jess had been trying to get her to date more mature men through the website boomers.com, but Tina hated every guy Jess picked out for her.

"Yes, Marlon," Jessica chimed in. "He was the one who turned out to be gay, if I remember correctly. Who of us hasn't had that experience? They're kind, generous, good listeners, and have good taste in clothing so you don't have to get them ready for public. All of it too good to be true ... and it is!" She took a long swig of her wine, emptying the glass.

"Yeah, but it took Sister Nun a long, long time to realize she was dating a gay guy," Tina stated emphatically. "Anyone else would have high-stepped it out of that relationship when the brother was reading all of the E. Lynn Harris novels before she even got a chance to know the next one had been published." E. Lynn Harris, an openly gay man, was a popular fiction author whose characters were either on the down-low or closeted gay men.

"That's not fair. It wasn't that obvious." Wine spurting out their mouths, Tina and Jessica just missed each other with the liquid. Laughter reached a record pitch.

"Okay, he did have a guy roommate for five years and used to brag about cooking the best Sunday brunches for all of his guy friends, and he did start crying when he wasn't able to hook up with his mentor from Morehouse when we were at that conference. But it wasn't long after the crying spree before I figured it out." Tina fell off the couch laughing.

"It was only nine months." I stamped my foot and stood, arms akimbo. Their laughter continued. "Well, maybe a year." I joined the laughter and was very glad that those days were behind me. I hoped that my gaydar had improved.

"Hey, I redeemed myself with Jon," I said, once we all could gain our composure.

"Yeah, White Guy is not so bad." Tina adored her brother-in-law, and Jon equally loved and enjoyed Tina.

"You did all right, Kathy. You finally kissed your prince," Jessica said with a hint of jealousy in her voice. She had always been a diehard romantic whom Tina teased relentlessly for her fantasy creations of what married life could and would be.

"You will too, Jess. Don was just one frog, and you do have to close one door fully before you can open up another." I gave her a hug as she began to look despondent.

"Hey, I thought you weren't playing psychologist tonight," Tina barked.

"I'm not. That message goes out from one sister to another." I glanced at the clock which indicated that it was well past midnight.

"Yikes. Look what time it is. You know I like to go to bed on the same day I got up on, and that is what I will be doing. You guys can continue your all-night Mother Love chat."

"No, we're all done, too. I've got to get going. I have to be in the studio by eleven; so I need to catch a few winks if I'm going to be coherent." Jessica shuffled to the other side of the room, placed her feet into her peep-toe heels that lay near the coat tree, grabbed her Burberry rain coat, and turned to give us both a swift kiss on the cheek.

"You okay going home, Jess? You're welcome to stay here." Tina offered as she rested her hand on Jessica's shoulder.

"Yeah, I'm cool. Thanks, anyway. I need to get to my place. Kath, thanks again for the interview and have a safe flight back to Cleveland." With another round of kisses, Jessica exited. Tina and I watched as she pulled out of the driveway still exchanging waves and blowing more kisses.

"Let's get this kitchen cleaned up. It won't take long with both of us doing it," I said to Tina as we took the few steps to the kitchen that was visible from the living room.

Despite the late hour, having everything in its rightful place was a habit embedded in all of the Carpenter sisters by our mom Sheila, and within an hour Tina's loft once again looked like a model home ready for a showing.

"This was a great evening, Tina. I think all the girl talk may have done Jessica some good."

"Yeah, Sister Nun, I hope she can get her groove back soon." We hugged good night.

A quick and welcomed shower allowed my body to get in the bed with relaxed muscles. Pulling down the white down comforter in Tina's guest room, I glanced around appreciating her talent. The mirrored chest of drawers was a perfect complement to the fresh, clean decor. I turned over to face the window, the warmth of my favorite paisley pajamas under the thick duvet covers adding to my comfort—a comfort that was suddenly disturbed when I heard Tina's scream that could have shattered one of the mirrored chests.

Later, I could not recall how I made it to Tina's bedroom so quickly, but I will always remember Tina's face when she looked at me with the phone held loosely in her hand.

"Don is dead," she cried.

CHAPTER 2A

It took us only twelve minutes to make the twenty-minute trip to Jessica's condo in the Buckhead area. I quickly pulled into the paved area in front of her door, and Tina jumped out, barely allowing me to brake. Having seen the headlights pull up to her garage, Jessica was at the front door in a nanosecond, just as Tina instantly flung it open. There was no attempt made to mask her wild grief. Even after her mother died, Jessica grieved with composure. Witnessing her in this horrid state was more than disconcerting. The polished news anchor speech that typically could convey deep emotion in a sentence without shocking an audience was gone. She was a complete mess. Putting my discomfort aside, I quickly moved into psychologist mode.

"Jess, honey, come, let's sit down." I guided Jessica to the full-grain leather sofa while Tina followed, weeping uncontrollably. She was proving to be little support to Jessica tonight.

"Iiii... wan... him... to... come... baaack. Ohhh... my God!

Oh, my God!" Jessica gulped and began to choke as she swallowed her tears.

"Jess, sweetie, take a breath," I instructed. She did not heed my direction and sobbed even louder while attempting to talk to us.

"Ittt…was…soo…horri…ble. Oh, my God…Oh, my God!"

"Shh…Shh…there is no need to say anything. I want you to just breathe. Deep, deep breaths from down here." I pointed to my diaphragm. Surprisingly, Jessica paid attention and made an attempt to focus on her breathing.

"Tina, please get Jess some water." Tina stood in front of us staring stoically, her eyes resembling a deer before headlights. I'm surprised she wasn't more hysterical, but I guess she didn't need to be because Jessica was doing enough emoting for all of us.

"Tina!" I repeated. She jumped. I intentionally lowered my voice. "Please go get some water for Jessica and drink some yourself, okay Sis." Understandably, they were both a complete mess.

We sat as a threesome on the couch. Sandwiched between Jessica and Tina, who were now a bit calmer, my tears made their way down my face. Tina reached over and dabbed one of them with a tissue.

"I just can't cry anymore. And I've run out of tissue." Jessica's voice approached a subdued yet somewhat normal tone.

"Don't worry. No one has ever drowned of tears." I reassured her. "And toilet paper is as good as Kleenex."

"Jess, how did it happen?" I asked as Tina moved to the carpeted floor and sat cross-legged in front of Jessica, pulling the end of her trench coat over her red silk nightshirt, her eyes bugging out slightly.

"Oh, God. That's the horrible part. He fell to his death..." Jess's tears began again, but she kept talking.

"... off the balcony." Jessica's voice was barely audible.

Tina pulled herself to her knees facing Jess. "This is either a really bad dream or I am in some fucking *Law & Order* episode."

"Tina..." I couldn't help myself. It was an automatic response to the F word, although it did feel like a *Law & Order* television episode, and I had seen just about all of them.

"Oh, gosh Jess, from the balcony?"

Jessica paused and appeared to be deep in thought. "Actually, I really don't know how he fell off the balcony."

"He must have been drinking and out bankrolling. I knew this would..."

"Tina, please." I interrupted, shaking my head and directing attention to Jessica. "Let's not go there tonight."

"Where else is there to go, Kath? Don was all caught up in that stuff. It's what broke up their relationship." Tina turned to Jessica and pleaded for her to agree.

"By the way, it's two o'clock in the morning. How did you find this out?" Best to shift the discussion to just sharing facts.

"Somebody posted it on Facebook." Tina sarcastically responded while giving Jessica a penetrating look.

Jessica sat in silence for what felt like at least five minutes. "Uh…one of the producers called me and told me that the story came across the wire. He didn't want me to hear it on the…" She stared at the carpet, examining the thick strands as if they were blades of grass she had just freshly cut with a mower. "Anyway, it doesn't matter how I found out. He's gone. He was out of my life before this, but now he's gone for good. I can't believe it." She began to cry again. "I know. I know." Tina relented and pulled Jessica into a tight hug. And the only thing I knew to do at that point was to join them.

CHAPTER 2B

Kathy actually came to a full halt at the stop sign, and there wasn't a ride in sight at this hour of the morning. If I made a federal case out of her driving, it wouldn't get us to Jess's condo any sooner. Better that two more people do not die tonight, and besides, I needed to calm myself in order not to make it a fourth. I could kill Jessica myself for being so stupid... so stupid. How could she have got herself so wrapped up in this man knowing all that she knew? She needs to get on program, keep her mouth zipped, and move on. We both needed to move on.

"Tina! Be careful!" Kathy's mom voice carried as I descended from the car, viewing Jessica's image framing the door. Grabbing Jessica, I got a flash scene of Queen Latifah and Jada Pickett embracing each other before Latifah's character goes off to die in that movie, *Set it Off.* Only this was real life. How did it come to this? Somebody better wake me up from this nightmare soon.

"Jess, honey, come, let's sit down." Kathy was doing her

Dr. Phil thing. Oh, my God, this isn't a dream. Kathy is here and in full nun psychologist mode.

"Iii … wan … him … to come … baaack. Ohhh … my God! Oh my God!" Jessica choked just in time. Don't tell her anything, Jess. Don't tell her anything, Jess.

"Jess, sweetie, take a breath." Kathy sounded like a yoga instructor, and maybe if she put Jess in one of those yoga positions that inverted her body over her head, she wouldn't end up talking about what happened.

"Itt … was … soo … horri … ble. Oh, my God … Oh, my God!" Jess was about to spill it all just like she did on the phone. No one, not even Kathy, would understand why she needed to go to try to see him in the middle of the night, especially when he ends up dead. Keep it to yourself, girlfriend. I peered into Jessica's tear-filled eyes hoping to connect on the message that no one is requiring you to say anything.

"Shh … Shh … there is no need to say anything." Damn, I knew Kathy was good at this shrink stuff, but was she reading my mind?

"I want you to just breathe. Deep, deep breaths from down here." Oh, she's just prepping her to talk coherently. Kathy pointed to her diaphragm as I mouthed "Shut Up!" to Jessica who returned a puzzled look. Obviously she hadn't connected the dots that it might not be a good thing to let people know that you actually saw your ex-fiancé plunge to his death. Jess, please use your smarts on this one. Jess, please use your smarts. Begging the energy of my thoughts to throttle Jessica's vocal chords, I continued to stare at her.

"Tina, please get Jess some water." Kathy was still playing Dr. Phil and now she was Mother Theresa. I didn't want to leave the room and have Jessica start filling in details. I'm no attorney, but I told her to never breathe a word of what she said to me on the phone to anyone. I neglected to tell her that included Sister Nun.

"Tina!" Damn, Kathy's loud voice was most likely interrupting my telepathic communication with Jessica.

"Please go get some water for Jessica and drink some yourself, okay, Sis." Water? Water? Don's brain had just been splattered on some concrete slab, and Sister Nun wanted me to go get water instead of tequila. Kath's so damn smart and emotionally intuitive even though she's so simple in the streets stuff. I've got no choice but to shut my mouth and get the water. Giving Jess my best mom-teacher-pastor-don't-you-even-think-about-it stare, I quickly went to the kitchen.

Within a minute I continued my now perfected stare and placed the glass of water on the end table next to Jessica. Luckily she was only crying and not talking. Kathy sat next to her, rubbing her back in that one-hundred-and-fifty-dollars-an-hour-therapist kind of way. She was now crying, and it made me feel guilty that I didn't want Kath to know the full truth, but once she knew the full truth, that toothpaste would be out of the tube without a chance in hell of getting it back in. Kathy would never be able to act as if she didn't know the full truth. Damn, she would probably go to confession, and some priest would encourage her to turn Jessica and me in to the police. Reaching for a tissue, I reminded myself that this was not a dream and found myself dabbing Kathy's tears to confirm that she was really there.

"I just can't cry anymore. I've run out of tissue." Jess was no longer crying, and that couldn't be good. She would want to share.

"Don't worry. No one has ever drowned of tears. And toilet paper is as good as Kleenex." Kathy sounded genuinely empathetic despite the fact that she'd probably said that same line to about a million patients.

"Jess, how did it happen?" Oh no, Kathy was going to go there. I plunged to the floor, crossing my legs and exposing their bareness, as my red silk nightshirt crept its way up around my waist.

"Oh, God. That's the horrible part. He fell to his death..." Big mouth, Jess. I could have taken what she knew to my grave.

"He fell from the balcony..." Jessica continued, then immediately hesitated. Thankfully, she felt the energy from my stare and looked directly at me. I made a quick slash to the throat gesture.

Kathy quickly turned to look at me. "This is either a really bad dream or I am in some fucking *Law & Order* episode." I quickly said, hoping that the F word would distract her.

"Tina..." It worked. Kathy was programmed to say my

name every time I said the F word, and intentionally using it interrupted the flow of conversation.

"Jess, is that how it really happened?" Kathy was such a persistent little pest.

Jessica paused and appeared to be deep in thought. "Actually I really don't know how he fell off the balcony."

"He must have been drinking and out bankrolling. I knew this would…" I couldn't help myself. If Jessica was going to talk about Don as if he was probably gazing at the stars when he fell to his death, somebody had to put it in context.

"Tina, please." Kathy interrupted me in an attempt to get me to be more sensitive to what we all already knew was the truth. "Let's not go there."

"Where else is there to go, Kath? Don was all caught up in that stuff. It's what broke up their relationship." Jessica better back me up on this one. If she wasn't convinced of that after tonight, I would need to get Kathy to admit her to the loony bin.

"By the way, it's two o'clock in the morning. How did you find this out?" Kathy was like a cockroach when it came to getting information. She never lost her train of thought—no matter how you tried to throw her off track, you couldn't stop that train.

"Somebody posted it on Facebook." I quickly responded and gave Jessica a look once again to say don't you dare even tell her.

Jessica sat quietly. She was used to reading the news from

the teleprompter but not making stuff up. "Uh … one of the producers called me and told me that the story came across the wire. He didn't want me to hear it on the …" Not bad for an amateur and definitely plausible. Good girl, Jess.

"Anyway, it doesn't matter how I found out. He's gone. He was out of my life before this, but now he's gone for good. I can't believe it." Jessica began to cry again.

"I know. I know." Despite the fact that I hated his guts for what he had done to her and often thought he would be better off dead, Jessica was my best friend and had just lost someone she still deeply loved. I gave her the tightest hug I could as Kathy's arms wrapped around us both.

CHAPTER 3

In full swing designer mode, Tina matched the paint swatches to carpet samples on the floor of the sanctuary at St. Monica Augustine. She refused to stop at my house when I picked her up at Cleveland Hopkins Airport just an hour ago. Grant it, we had lost over a week on this redecorating project for Fr. Randy's twenty-fifth ordination anniversary, but the furor with which she was working on the remodeling now was nerve-racking. Tina swearing in the sanctuary over paint colors and her perfectionism causing other people to swear would be quite the scene. Not that anybody cared about Tina using obscenities in general, but they would care if she couldn't control her language in the sanctuary. When she was in Designer Sergeant Mode, all bets were off.

"So, tell me about Don's funeral." I sat in the first pew of the empty church and leaned forward, watching as she obsessively went back and forth with paint swatches on the wall by the wood carved plaque of the Holy Family.

Tina stopped and reflected. "It wasn't much of a home

going, if you ask me…oh, you just did." Tina laughed at her own joke. "I had to ask Fr. Mark from Our Lady of Lourdes to do the funeral Mass and burial. Thank God that he agreed to do it because nobody else would bless Don's sorry ass. No one knew of any funds to get his body back to Cleveland to bury him here where at least there would be some family… ghetto as they all are. But at least somebody could have been there for him. None of his blood family even made it to the funeral. They were all there when he was rolling in dough; now they all scattered, scared they might have to pay his bills."

"What happened to all of his buddies? I thought when he and Jess were together, he was just as popular in the Atlanta crowd." Don was strikingly handsome with a gregarious personality that might have been a bit foolhardy at times, but never offensive. I couldn't imagine Jessica being with anyone who wasn't personable.

"That is just it. Despite the fact that he was always very generous with his friends and giving them all these lavish gifts after he lost his money, they all disappeared. They didn't come back until he hooked up with Jess and fed off him just to get to Jess, thinking they could get a media hook-up. Superficial jerks couldn't even make one last showing for his funeral." Tina resumed paging through a large paint sample catalogue, typically only seen in Lowe's or Home Depot. Tina had her personal copy shipped to St. Monica Augustine from Atlanta.

"What do you think about this?" She extended a smoky

blue paint swatch. "I think this looks heavenly." Tina often asked and answered her own questions about decorating. She continued without waiting for my response, not really caring what I thought anyway.

"It was just me and Jessica and a few of her friends from the station who knew she was pretty messed up. They were there to support her. Actually, I take that back—some of his work friends were there, and there were a few people from Cleveland. They could have been relatives. And I think that white woman he was cheating on Jess with was hovering in the back with this cute gay guy. She had on huge sunglasses and a floppy hat and kept holding on to this tall black chick and the gay guy. I don't think Jess saw her, and I wasn't about to point her out. Wasn't the time or place, and she was pretty pissed at me for even mentioning any possibility of cheating the first time, so I wasn't having her go off on me again. Besides, I wasn't sure if it was the same woman. I just knew she was white, and it's a good possibility it was her." Tina paused, as if to count how many white women Don could have possibly known well enough to attend his funeral.

"So, all in all, there was maybe about thirty, forty folks altogether and even fewer at the burial. It was just all really sad."

"Gosh, that is sad. Any more info about how he died? Nobody really talks about that." My imagined visual of Don falling from a balcony and then hitting a slab of concrete remained a vivid picture.

"I guess he must have been drinking, or that's what everyone assumes. He probably broke his neck or cracked open his head." Tina shivered. "I really don't want to know any details."

"You're right. Among all of the ways to go, it is probably high on the list of worst ways to die." Reflecting on the thought brought Jessica to mind. "How's Jessica doing?"

"Okay. I think. I talked to her right before I left for the…" Tina stopped and let out a happy yell. "Hey, Fr. What-A-Waste!" She watched Randy walk down the aisle. "We're going to have your pad ready for some real church up… in… here!" Tina gave Randy a high-five as they laughed and embraced.

"How's it going, sisters?" Randy, dressed in black shirt and pants with white clerical collar loosened, reached over and planted a brisk kiss on my cheek. He must have returned from parish business, otherwise his uniform Dockers pants and polo shirt would have been the attire.

"When did you get in, Tina?" He picked up some of the samples Tina had strewn on the floor, and I knew Tina would start having a hissy fit if he messed up the order in what might look like disarray to an unsuspecting non-designer.

"We've only been here about an hour." I offered. "By the way, Tina's entourage arrives tomorrow."

The expression on Randy's face indicated that he didn't remember the conversation we had when I returned from Atlanta and reported to him the change of plans. Refusing to trust that any painter with whom she hadn't previously work could make the deadline, Tina insisted on having her own painting crew complete the work. Consequently, Modell and Ronny were flying in tomorrow on the Carpenter family's dime. It was worth it just to have Tina work the way she needed to complete the redesign. When the designer was happy, everyone was happy. As a result, Tina ended up completing the project in record time and the results were miraculous.

"Wow! What an improvement, Tina. Too bad there isn't an *Extreme Church Makeover* television show. You could take your skills on the road." Jon walked with us into St. Monica Augustine. We had arrived early, knowing that the ordination celebration would draw standing room-only crowd for the ten thirty Mass, not only because there was such genuine love for Randy, but because there was a catered brunch after Mass. Anything that was distributed for free, whether it was ashes for Ash Wednesday, palm branches on Palm Sunday, or especially food for any occasion seemed to draw a large crowd to St. Monica Augustine.

By the time the choir sang a rousing rendition of Byron Cage's "The Presence of the Lord," the church was packed. Ushers placed folding chairs in every available nook and cranny.

The Spirit of the Lord is here... It had been ages since I had seen Randy's grandmother who sat proudly with his mother in the front pew. Randy's family, even with his influence, were not regular church-goers and would never convert to Catholicism. They remained "just God-fearing lovers of people who wants to do the right thing in life," as Randy's mother would explain it when someone asked about her parish membership. "Besides, we gots all the Jesus in Randy that we need."

I feel it in the atmosphere... The parish Youth Group marched with the Wisdom Council in the processional up to the altar representing the past, present, and future of St. Monica Augustine.

The power of the Lord is here... Bishop Collins, along with several priests from Randy's order, took their seats in the sanctuary. Pastors Toby and Richard Sloan from the nearby Presbyterian Church, friends, and community partners with Randy joined the clergy. Mayor Andrew Marvan and Cleveland's First Lady, Sandra Marvan, clapped enthusiastically while smiling at Cleveland's business and education leaders, Paxton Broussard, John Barnstable, and Patrick Simpson, seated across the aisle.

A blessing from the Lord is here... As Randy led the Sign of the Cross, "In the name of the Father, the Son, and the Holy Spirit," my sister Dana, her husband Darien, and my niece and nephew, Portia and Wayne, squeezed into the pew with us.

"You wouldn't believe how many people I had to butt whip out of this pew trying to save your seats." Tina loudly whispered to Dana, who simply chuckled. If my mom Sheila weren't up front with the Wisdom Council, she would be hushing Tina and Dana right now, reminding me of when we were in elementary school.

After repeated verses of the opening song, the congregation moved quickly through the introductory rites to the sermon preached by Fr. Tony Mallozzi, Randy's seminarian classmate. He wove in a bit of black Catholic history and provided inspiration from the life of the Reverend Augustus Tolton, the nation's first-known black Roman Catholic priest who, he informed us, may soon be canonized as St. Augustus. He jokingly predicted that the canonization of Fr. Randy would follow shortly after that.

The two-hour liturgy was considered long even by St. Monica Augustine standards and clearly way over the typical fifty minutes that characterized the time it took for Mass in most parishes, particularly those with predominately white congregants. No one seemed to mind or attempted to rush to their cars after Holy Communion, but instead the crowd moved quickly into the church hall for a catered waffle and chicken brunch in thanksgiving and fellowship.

"You know, the first African American priests were actually three brothers who were born to a slave woman in Georgia and her Irish immigrant master," Jon remarked as he generously poured syrup over his waffle. Jon was noted to know more black history than any white man alive.

"How can that be? And where did you hear that?" Dana queried.

"No, no, it's true. They were sent up north and passed for white. One ended up being the first president of Georgetown University around the mid-1870s, which at the time wasn't even accepting black students." Jon reached for another chicken wing from the buffet-style servings in the middle of the table.

"You ought to go on *Jeopardy*." Portia said. Portia was fascinated with the quiz show, envied her uncle's fund of knowledge, and had a not-so-secret wish to be on the show herself.

Darien finally made it to the table after making his rounds visiting some old high school friends who came into town.

"I didn't realize that Archie and Jim were connected to St. Monica Augustine. They told me they used to play basketball here as a teen. That's really something. Small world. They knew Randy from when he was a seminarian, and Randy used to coach them! Must have been some award-winning team with Randy as their coach," Darien threw his head back and laughed. "That's real nice, though. They've got most of the guys from his first team here and even took a picture lined up the way they were twenty-five years ago. It's a class reunion over there. I remember a lot of those guys."

"One of them lives in Atlanta now," Tina glanced over at the table.

"Who?" I asked simply out of curiosity not expecting to be able to identify any of them.

"The good-looking gay guy at the end of the table facing us," Tina replied.

"How do you know he's gay?" It was a question I would typically ask, but Dana beat me to it.

"Modell recognized him when he came into the church looking for Randy when we were painting. He knew him from the clubs, and Modell has a memory like an elephant when it comes to remembering fine-looking men. We were both sizing him up, and Modell said 'Forget it Tina, he's a DL brother.'" Tina laughed.

"DL?" I thought aloud.

"Down-Low, Aunt Kathy." Wayne quickly educated me.

"I knew that." I attempted to rescue myself from the ridicule I was sure to experience in the moments to come. My family was merciless when it came to teasing me about my lack of knowledge about black pop culture.

Randy approached the table and fist-bumped Wayne while taking the seat next to him. Thanking God for the rescue from ridicule, I listened as Randy engaged the family with humorous stories about some of the people in the room. Darien cajoled that he didn't know what he was more impressed about—the fact that Randy once was a basketball coach, or that his first team showed up to honor him.

"Well, it certainly wasn't because of my coaching talent. Actually, I think all of them are here only partially because of me. The occasion provided a good opportunity for them to get together. Many of them knew Don Davenport; although he wasn't on the team, he hung around a lot. When something like that happens, it causes folks to want to make a special effort to get together because it's a reminder that life is way too short."

"Wow, I didn't realize you knew Don. You didn't mention it when we talked about his passing," I said, trying to sort out some confusion.

"I didn't know him. At least, I don't remember him at all. Jamal, one of the guys, and some of the others did. Jamal knew him pretty well and even tried to help in out in recent years, finding him a job and helping him keep focused. They tell me Don was really more of a pseudo-thug back then. He was the kind of guy that was popular with the ladies and was considered to be a bit of a jerk, but a friendly jerk, to most of the guys. Really smart and would do anything for anybody." Randy turned and glanced back at the table referencing Jamal and catching his attention. Jamal interpreted Randy's glance as a request to come over to the table. His honey complexion, muscular torso, and devilish grin anchored by his deep dimples evoked attention from all of us at the table. Jamal wrapped an arm over Randy's left shoulder.

"Excuse me," Jamal said to us as he interrupted. "Fr. Randy, I'm going to roll on out of here. I'm glad that I came. Congratulations, man!"

Randy turned and embraced him. "Hey, take care of yourself, and if you need to talk, you know where to find me." Our entire table made no attempt to disguise our eavesdropping.

"I may take you up on that. Life is so fragile, and you never know what might happen. Living with regrets weighs on you more than I could ever imagine. You know I had just seen Don hours before..." Tucking his chin into his chest, he gave a heavy pat on Randy's shoulder, looked up, and silently nodded a final goodbye as he left the room.

We all sat staring at Randy; even Jon stopped sucking on a chicken wing.

"He's pretty broken up about his friend, and he's got some other things going on in his life."

"If he needs someone to comfort him, I would be happy to provide a corporal work of mercy." Tina's uncanny knack for conveniently recalling Catholic school catechism was self-serving.

Randy laughed and knew better not to take Tina's bait. "Anyway, it is good that the guys came; a little bonding and reminiscing are good for everybody," Randy reflected and then pointed to Darien. "Hey, believe it or not, we're going to get a game together tomorrow; so Darien and Jon, it's on if you want to join us and judge my skills. The rest of you can take bets."

After profusely thanking Tina and our family for the remodel, Randy gave each of us a warm embrace as he moved to greet and visit his other guests. A lot of love in this room surrounded him—a real testimony to his selfless, generous spirit that had touched and enriched the lives of so many.

"I'm glad he liked the remodel." Tina placed two more

chicken wings on the remaining quarter of the waffle square. At fifty years old, Tina could eat half a side of beef and still weigh the same as she did when she was half her age.

"It turned out fabulous, Tina! In record time, you pulled it together. Did you hear the Wisdom Council oohing and ahhing..." Mom began to praise her daughter just as sounds of a reggae ring tone interrupted.

"That's yours, Tina." Dana instructed.

Tina pulled her large, black suede Ghibli bag on the table, reaching in to silence the ringing phone that was barely audible over the noise in the church hall.

"Oh, it's Jess." She said and decided to take the call.

"Tell her hi and give her our love," Mom shouted over to Tina from her place at the head of the table.

"Jess, I can't hear you. What did you say?" Tina pressed her forefinger on the fold of her ear to hear Jessica better.

"You might want to go outside to get a better reception," Darien offered. His advice wasn't necessary, for we heard Tina's frantic tone that belied her words of comfort. "Don't worry, Jess. I'll leave now and get the next flight home." She hung up and stared blankly into the space before her as if she were the only person in the room.

"Is everything okay?" I gingerly asked.

"No, no." Tina began to cry. "Jessica's been taken in for questioning about her involvement in the murder of Don Davenport."

CHAPTER 4

The party center that was chosen for Regina Academy's Class of 1988 twenty-fifth class reunion received only three out of five stars on internet reviews, but there were other positives for consideration. The price was right, and although average, the food was tasty and filling. And everyone in the class knew where the suburb of Belden was located. The party center owner was a graduate of Regina Academy, and virtually every school social and fundraiser had been held there in order to take advantage of the hefty discount. Adding to the ease of executing the reunion, all of the committee members lived in Belden, some raising their families on the same street as their childhood home. Three of the committee members were now sending their sons and daughters to Regina Academy, since it conveniently became co-ed just four years ago. Belden was a bit of a make-believe Pleasantville community that lacked the edginess of an urban environment that under normal circumstances I might find somewhat boring, but given the whirlwind schedule of the book tour, the influx of very needy patients to my clinical practice, and most immediately, Tina and Jessica's upset over Don Davenport's mysterious death, Pleasantville was welcomed in my life.

"I still find it amusing that we are actually going to this reunion." Jon, interrupting my thoughts, turned a sideways glance at me while taking the exit on Route 271S heading toward Kate's Party Center. "You've done nothing but fuss about how you are not prepared physically or emotionally for it."

I frowned a bit. Jon was right. He generally was. But I was just caught up in the everyday when I did all that fussing. Right now I really needed this reunion as a distraction.

"Well, I only lost five pounds and wanted to lose about twenty." I chuckled as I thought about the stacks of one hundred-calorie packaged foods in the kitchen pantry. "And emotionally... well, it just feels like things are on hold with life since Jess's been implicated."

"She'll be okay. She's got the best legal counsel, and you and Tina both say there's nothing against her, and they were just asking routine questions. They aren't even sure it was a murder. Sometimes, police work is just a matter of adding some drama for the media. A broken relationship with an ex-fiancé who nearly bankrupted her... It's all good drama."

Jon turned his attention away from the road when he heard my deep sigh. "It's natural that they would probe a bit and ask Jessica questions. She had to know more about him than any other person. It will all die down shortly, if it hasn't already." It was the millionth time that Jon had gone over this logical argument crafted to reduce my anxiety. He was right again. After being questioned for hours, Jessica was not considered a suspect, but the police remained vigilant and had continued an official investigation for the past month. That was the part I still found unnerving.

I glanced at Jon and another deep sigh left my body. Believing that going to my class reunion would be a good distraction from worrying about Jess only exchanged one anxiety for another. The last time I saw most of my classmates was at the tenth-year reunion when I was still in the convent.

"Seeing my former classmates might be a bit awkward." I looked fondly over at Jon. "At least introducing you can be a conversation starter."

"It won't be the first time that I have been used in this relationship," Jon said as he skillfully parked the Acura at the party center between an SUV and a large sedan with its wheels turned inward straddling the white line.

Exiting the car, we walked toward the door as Jon sang the old Bill Withers song from the movie *Lean on Me.* "You can just…lean on me when you're not strong. I'll be your friend. I'll help you carry on."

He held the handle of the glass door for me to enter. I laughed and was conveniently smiling as we approached the registration table which I was relieved to see was positioned only two hundred feet from the entrance so we didn't have to wander around and mingle right away.

"Oh. My. God." Marcie Johnson quickly scooted from

behind the table and in an instant wrapped her arms around me, squeezing me so hard the silver beads around my neck uncomfortably plunged into my throat. "When I see you on TV, I scream and tell my kids, 'I know her, I went to school with her.' They say, 'We know, Mom. You've told us that a hundred times. Who cares?' Well, I tell them I do. I care. I know someone famous."

"Well, I wouldn't say famous." I tried to minimize any claim for celebrity, but Marcie was already handing Sandy Matthews her phone and instructing her how to use the camera function.

"Let me get a picture before everyone else grabs you, so I can show those kids. They'll believe me now."

I grabbed Jon and included him in the shot. Marcie didn't object and politely nodded when I quickly introduced him as my husband. She looked as if to quiz me, "Do you know he's white?" I gave her a look back that told her I was well aware that Jon was indeed a white man.

"Here's your name tag and your keepsake book." Sandra handed both articles to me and smiled. "I'm glad you came. With your celebrity you've added some panache to the reunion."

"You're very sweet, Sandy." I gave her a hug. Sandy was voted most congenial and obviously still could earn the award. "These nametags are very clever," I said to both Sandy and Marcie as I showed it to Jon. Our high school picture was positioned on one end of the tag, and at the other end, our first name stood in bold capital letters with the last name in smaller font underneath.

"I love the Jheri curl." Jon pointed to the glossy, loose curls that framed my youthful face.

"What do you know about Jheri curls?" I asked, amazed at Jon's fund of knowledge on black culture. He almost got a chance to respond, but we were interrupted by a series of squeals from the girls of the Regina Academy journalism club. Although I wasn't a part of the school's newspaper staff, as a member of the journalism club, I had worked on the annual yearbook. I actually recognized the faces of the women approaching me. One of them held a copy of the *You and Your Partner* series.

"This is not at all as I imagined this reunion," I whispered to Jon as the journalism girls descended upon me. "What made me think they wouldn't remember me?" If the floor opened up and suctioned me into the ground, the grave would be met with gratitude.

"Uh, to start, I think being the only black kid in the class might make you memorable," Jon whispered back as I ignored the obvious truth of his statement. "And, honey, like it or not, your work puts you in the forefront."

"Hi," I sheepishly greeted the journalism club girls. My voice sounded strange even to me, and I made an effort to swallow in order to appear as confident as my classmates obviously believed me to be. I pulled Jon to my side and put on a smile from ear to ear.

The gawking journalism girls formed a semi-circle around me.

"This is my husband, Jon," I pulled him closer into the inner sanctum.

"Hi," he echoed as the journalism girls continued to stare and gawk.

Hoping to break their stupors, I threw out a general question. "Well, tell me about what's going on in your worlds now?"

They continued to stare.

"Jackie?" I coached the woman to my right after conveniently reading Jackie Adams on her name tag.

"Well, I'm married," she gushed, happy to be picked first to speak. "I have three kids. My husband, Mitchell, is over there with all the other guys." She pointed to the corner, and the rest of the women giggled and nodded.

"Oh, all of your husbands are also friends. How nice!" I sincerely meant that. I was glad to be in Pleasantville. Kelly Niemen handed me her book with a pen and I made the correct assumption that she wanted me to sign it. It was the *When Mental Illness Separates* book from the *You and Your Partner* series. Yikes. I hoped that she had just picked up a random copy for me to sign. Which one of the men over there was her husband with a mental disorder? Not one of the women moved an inch as I penned my name on the interior title page.

"Yeah, all the husbands gets along really good. All our kids do too." Darcy Wynn proudly proclaimed. With her use of grammar, I wondered how she could have possibly gotten into the journalism club. Maybe she did graphics.

"So, you're all married, have kids, live in … Belden." I took a guess on the location.

"No, everyone but me lives in Belden. I live in Clinton." Debra Cato glanced at me and must have interpreted my surprise as disappointment. "It's on the border of Belden," she offered apologetically. "My husband Bill's family lived there, so it was close for raising the kids. You know, easy babysitters then, but all my kids are grown now. We just never moved. Now we can babysit for their kids."

I gulped. Did my classmates really have grandkids already? "That's really nice, but I can't imagine …" Someone had grabbed my neck in a choke hold. I pleaded with my eyes for Jon to help me out, but he was enjoying this all too much.

"You get three clues and first two don't count," a familiar voice said.

"Jon, make sure you get this woman's name so we can sue her for assault."

"You always were such a smart ass." Sr. Joy Marie released her grip and warmly gave me a hug.

"Joy Marie!" I glanced at her name tag which read Joyce "Joy" Tucker. "Did you leave the convent?" I quickly asked. It had been over ten years since I left, and it would not surprise me at all if Joy had done likewise. She had never been particularly nun-like even in her early years as a postulant and novice.

"Yeah, I'm still a part of the community. But I'm no longer Catholic."

"That must be a joke." It took very little time for Joy and me to resume the lighthearted nature of our past relationship. She was obviously messing with me. Or maybe she wasn't? Her naturally arched eyebrow became slightly elevated and a sideways glance claimed otherwise. Were there actually nuns these days that weren't practicing Catholics?

"It's a long story. We can't get into it tonight," she looped her arm into mine and squeezed. "Kathy, you're the only reason why I even showed up to this gig. I called someone on the committee to find out if you were coming before I sent back my RSVP. You know nuns still attend for free... actually the cost of your ticket serves to subsidize my attendance so thank you very much. You won't regret your contribution for I intend to indulge a bit tonight." Jon let out a quick laugh.

"I'll go get drinks for everyone. Wine? White? Red?" He offered.

"Rum and Coke for me, thanks," Joy responded and Jon repeated the laugh.

I gave Jon a wink as Joy and I headed for the buffet table. He was familiar with stories from the convent days that involved Joy Marie and her unconventional nun behavior. His favorite was when she cussed out the police officer for giving her a speeding ticket, then bartered with the municipal judge on the case to have it dismissed by promising admission to Regina Academy for his wayward daughter.

Joy filled one plate with cheese, pepperoni, salami, prosciutto, pizza squares, and marinated vegetables from the antipasto table. I could feel her staring at the salad that covered the right corner of my plate.

"I hope you haven't become one of those vegetable people. What do they call themselves, vegan?" She pronounced vegan to rhyme with begging.

I laughed. "No, the dessert table just looks really good, and I know that my sweet tooth will kick in soon, so I'm balancing my choices to attack that tiramisu."

"No problem with that here, still room for it all." We used to tease her for having a foul mouth like a truck driver and eating like one too. Despite her hefty appetite, her figure remained enviable and accentuated in the simple royal blue silk shift dress she wore with a single strand of pearls. Her hair pulled back in a low ponytail with a silver clip distinguished her simplicity from the up does of her former classmates in the room.

Conversation proved challenging over the ten-piece band playing the Motown sounds from the 1960s. "Is your family still living in Bratenahl?" I asked, recalling how the Tucker family's expansive lake property was deemed one of the most expensive homes in the Cleveland area.

"Actually Mom died two years ago after a wicked battle with cancer, and Dad just passed three months ago." Joy paused, fork positioned in the air as if the gesture represented the interruption in her life.

"Oh, gosh. I am so sorry. They couldn't have been much past retirement age."

"Mmmm...yeah. Mom was only sixty-nine when she passed, and Dad would have been seventy-five in December."

"Oh, gee." This was not the atmosphere for this kind of discussion, but Joy appeared to be somewhat matter-of-fact about it. Garlic permeated the air as Jon seated himself next to me with a plate of roast beef and eggplant parmesan.

"Not bad, not bad," Jon proclaimed in between chews. Joy sat directly across from me as I leaned in to continue our conversation.

"I am so sorry. That must be tough to lose both parents in a relatively short period of time. How are you doing?"

Joy looked at me curiously as if I just asked the strangest question in the world. "I am thinking about how to answer that. You know how complicated things were in my family. I miss my mom terribly. She was so sweet and yet such a pathetic wimp in so many ways. My relationship with my dad got even more business-like after Mom died. It was strange. I both admired and respected him while despising almost everything he stood for."

Unfortunately the room quieted, with soft jazz coming from the speakers as the band took a twenty-minute break. Suddenly I was speechless, just when the atmosphere in the room shifted to make a more intimate conversation possible. And there were no journalism girls in sight to redirect the conversation.

Jon came up for breath, furiously plowing down a representative sample of every food item on the buffet table. "From what I remember reading about him, those sentiments were true for a lot of people."

"Did you know my dad?" Joy questioned Jon.

"Only in writing—newspapers, magazines, internet. And of course, his bio always surfaced on the list of potential donors to tap for Lakeside University." Jon returned to his love affair with his plate.

"Jon's the provost at Lakeside." I offered to fill in the blank for Joy. She smiled.

The reunion committee ascended the stage, and Sandy Matthews grabbed the microphone, unintentionally sighing into it. The loud feedback got everyone's attention, and she quickly jumped back as if the microphone were attacking her.

"Oh, so sorry. Obviously I am not used to using one of these things, but it did get your attention." She flattened the front of her pink above-the-knee Georgette dress, rubbing out the offending creases. Standing erect and moving a few inches back, she continued on confidently without the microphone's feedback.

"We, your twenty-fifth Reunion Committee," she gestured to the rest of the eight women on stage, "want to thank you for coming. We really enjoyed getting together to plan this event, and we hope that you are having a good time?" She began the applause as the room erupted to join her.

Each of the members then took turns sharing messages

from former teachers and a classmate who was serving in the Navy, and they led a brief eulogy and announced a scholarship fund in memory of a classmate who lost her life to breast cancer.

"There's plenty more food. Doesn't Kate still do a great job?" The microphone was returned to Sandy who led us in applause again as Kate and her staff appeared in the doorway from the kitchen. "And be sure to take home your souvenir wine glasses that were hand-painted by our own Marcie Johnson." Three committee women shoved Marcie up to the microphone to receive credit. Marcie smiled shyly and nodded, grateful for the recognition.

The band resumed playing the hits of the '70s and '80s as the girls from Regina Academy, with and without partners, took over the dance floor. Joy stood up and rounded the table to meet me on the other side.

"Hey, listen. I am going to get going before I can't drive myself home. My mission has been accomplished connecting with you again. Do you think we could get together soon? I work in Geauga County." She handed me a card with the address of the community hospital in the area and her name emblazoned as president. "I'm in Bratenahl a lot these days at my parent's house. Rachel has come back home to," she mocked quotation marks, 'find herself.' She thinks she might want to get a divorce. You remember Rachel, don't you?"

"I do. I do." Nodding, Rachel's natural beauty and spunky

nature were hard to forget. "She gave your parents a real run for their money, if I remember."

"Well, she's still running with their money, but that's a story that requires more alcohol. I'll give you a call so we can get together. I mean that." She gave me a hug. "Now let's not say the 'let's do lunch thing' and never do it, okay?"

I was in enthusiastic agreement and pleased that she would want to rekindle our friendship. We exchanged email addresses and mobile numbers and locked the deal with another hug.

"I'll walk you to your car." John was already heading toward the door with Joy.

"You got yourself a good one." Joy winked over her shoulder and blew me a kiss.

"I did. I did." As I turned to make my way to the dessert table, the journalism girls with their husbands descended upon me. I met them with sheer delight.

CHAPTER 5A

"Hey, Sister Nun, how was your reunion?" Traffic was particularly heavy for the middle of the afternoon, and I didn't want to miss my turn. I remembered seeing the restaurant somewhere in this block and wondered where and if they had valet parking. Maybe not at noontime, I concluded.

"Sister Nun, the reunion? You went, didn't you?" Tina's bellow through the car's Bluetooth overlapped with the voice of the GPS lady.

"Oh, yeah. I went." I turned my attention back to the conversation with Tina. "It was much better than I ever expected. The committee put a lot of work into making it a nice affair. I even recognized most of the girls and got to hook back up with Joyce Tucker. Remember her? Her nun name was Sr. Joy Marie." Pulling into the small parking lot on the side of the restaurant and eyeing an open spot brought a triumphant smile to my face that I had successfully arrived even though I needed the assistance of GPS.

"You mean the nun with the gutter mouth is still there?

ed to freak me out going around cursing. Her parents had that big ass house on the lake, and didn't her sister marry some black man just to piss off her Archie Bunker father?"

"Yep, that was Joy." Joy's personality was hard to forget and her life circumstances easy to remember. "It's hard for me to believe she was still there as well, but she's pretty radical in many ways. She's gone rogue on the anything traditionally Catholic and spends her time with spirituality groups on Sundays who do things like drumming and hugging trees."

"You're kidding me."

"Well, maybe not the hugging trees part, but she did tell me about the drumming community she attends on Sundays. We've had lunch a couple of times since the reunion. She hasn't changed a bit."

"That's good. She was pretty cool for a nun and was never really wrapped up with nun-like thinking. You and Randy would have those lame conversations about the state of black America and the marginalization of black Catholics. Oh my God, when I think of Randy. What a waste of a good-looking man. What a waste. You know, you bringing up that nun is so funny. Not funny ha ha, but funny weird. I was just thinking about Joy the other day. I couldn't remember her real name, but that white chick that I was telling you about that showed up at Don's funeral sorta looked like her. You know Don's first wife was white, and he only dated white women for a long time. I really think Jess might have been the only black woman that Don ever dated."

"How is Jess doing? I need to give her a call."

"She would appreciate that. Every passing week is a good thing. No news is good news, as they say, but it's still unsettling that the case isn't closed. She's taking one day at a time."

Removing the key from the ignition ended our weekly conversation. "Listen, give Jess my love and tell her I will call her soon. I've got to go…just pulled up to the restaurant so we'll talk later."

Randy was uncharacteristically on time sitting at the booth of the popular eatery in the Ohio City area of Cleveland that would have been typically only fifteen minutes away from my private practice office.

"So sorry to be late—it took longer than I expected. The traffic was crazy for this time of day." Easily sliding down the leather seat, I positioned myself directly across from Randy who quickly closed down his smart phone and put it aside.

"No problem. You're actually on time. I had a meeting with one of our vendors who turns out to be not too far from here. So I got here early." He paused. "I know it must have surprised the heck out of you seeing me here. 'Oh, God, I must be really late.'" Randy threw up his hands in a frantic wave.

Of the numerous times we had met for lunch or dinner, Randy routinely arrived within a fifteen-minute time frame, finding me patiently, and sometimes not so patiently, waiting.

I chuckled at his imitation of an infraction of my punctuality vow.

"How's the food here? I figure you've been here before?" Cleveland's vast number of ethnic groups gave rise to a wonderful mixture of tempting restaurants. Balaton was one of them with a menu that boasted the best of Hungarian food.

"Joy actually introduced me to the place. She loves it because of the large portions." Randy smiled at my assessment that I knew would make him happy. "I thought you would appreciate that as well."

A round-faced woman dressed in a white button-down collared shirt and black pants with a gold-plated tag showing "Eva" spelled out in large block letters approached our table and with only two spoken words, "ready?" and "thanks," took our orders for chicken schnitzel.

"Who was that who answered the phone last night when I called?" I didn't recognize the voice of any one of the typical Monica Augustine parishioners that might have been hanging around at the rectory.

"Must have been Jamal. He's actually been at the house for a few days while he's in town."

"Jamal ... from the ordination party?" I spoke out loud. It would have been difficult to forget such a memorable face.

"Yeah, you remember correctly. He was one of the first team guys who lived in Atlanta."

"Got it. Tina recognized him or thought she did. Or maybe it was someone she knew that did." I said, as I remembered that he was the one identified to be on the down-low and wondered if Randy could confirm that about him.

"Yeah, he was one of the guys who knew Don Davenport and has been pretty out of sorts since his death ... struggling a lot. He obviously knew a side to Don that others were not familiar with. Turns out Don was the guy they used to called Nod because of his backward black hillbilly family. I remembered the family. Mom got in a fight right in the middle of Mass with an ex-husband, throwing punches and everything. Happened just before the offertory procession, so some folks thought it was some kind of crazy dance or biblical dramatization. We've laughed about that story before. It's one of the highlights of my time as a deacon. I just didn't connect that family with Don Davenport." Randy paused, taking apart the chicken with his fork and pushing it around in the wine sauce. "This is pretty good ... pretty good. Anyway, life's tough for Jamal. He's separated from his wife and his business is challenging, especially with the recession ... trying to figure things out, so reaching out. How are things with Jessica, by the way? Jamal mentioned the investigation was still underway."

"If it is, they no longer seem too interested in Jess's connection. At least that's our hope."

"Everything good?" Two more words came from Eva as she hurried by the table, barely pausing for an affirmative response before she moved on to take an order from another table. The tables had quickly filled as the noon hour continued with a mixture of suit-clad business professionals and safety-vested construction workers.

"That's good to hear. I know Jamal is convinced that his death was accidental and thinks some rookie policeman is trying to make a name for himself investigating this as if he's going to uncover the answer to the unsolved mystery."

"Interesting. I wonder if the rookie has something unknown to the public."

"According to Jamal, Don was in pretty deep, financially. Some legitimate losses with bad investments, others that were the result of pure gambles. But there was a side to this guy that apparently nobody really knew about. Jamal has lots of regrets about how he handled their relationship and wished he had reached out to him more to get professional help instead of trusting and believing that he got his act together. Apparently they had a violent argument over a business transaction and his last words were pretty harsh. You know how you remember your last words with the deceased."

"Gosh... he's in good company. Jessica was in so deep that she now regrets breaking off the engagement, as if their relationship could have saved him. Tina was pretty rough on him for the way she thought he was ruining Jessica's life, but her regrets were short-lived. She's just so glad that he's out of Jessica's life, even if he is dead."

"Dessert?" Eva had returned.

"No, thanks." Randy and I said simultaneously. Eva laid the check on the table with a gentle smile that softened her demeanor and revealed two low dimples. "No rush," the latter statement defying her typical economy of words.

"Are you stalking me?" Randy's face brightened when he saw Joy Marie, and recognizing her voice, I turned to greet her.

"This is so wild. I told Randy you were the one to introduce me to this place."

"As I live and breathe, if it isn't the Fr. Randall Starling. Why aren't you a bishop or a monsignor by now or something? Weren't they grooming you for that back in the day?" Joy skipped over the "gee, it's been years since we have seen each other. What's going on?" foreplay and got right to the heart of what she wanted to know about Randy.

"Hey, Joy. Good to see you." Randy stood and gave Joy a hug, and I followed with the same. We had just seen each other last week for the second time, having kept our promise of getting together after the reunion. "You have obviously done well rising to the top. I don't get out to Geauga County much, but everyone loves St. Bede's and credits your leadership. Look how far you've come."

"No, it's more like look how far Dad's money has gone in my case. I think the nuns were afraid that Dad would disinherit me if I wasn't placed in some kind of leadership position, and it certainly wasn't going to be within the community as any mother superior. I'm not very good at the ministry thing, but I can run an honest business and the business of healthcare these days keeps me out of trouble."

I shook my head, not wishing to debate Joy's seasoned leadership competencies that had propelled her to the top of her game in healthcare. Add to that her position as president of Catholic Health Care Administrators and its influence on health policy—both positions defied her stated diminished role in ministry.

"Hey, I was going to call you. I need a favor." Joy turned to me. "My sister really needs a shrink, and you're the only one I can get her even to come close to seeing."

"Uh... I'll talk to her about some good referrals. I think the relationship is a little too close for my comfort zone." Joy's brow creased. I tried to convince her. "You understand, Joy, I know too much of your family stuff, and we are just reviving our friendship."

"All the more reason." Joy was not buying my struggle with ethical boundaries, and I had no desire to convince her of my discomfort in a restaurant.

"We can talk more. We are on for lunch again next month, right?"

"Done?" Eva motioned for the folder where Randy had placed thirty-five dollars.

"Change?"

"Yours," Randy said. Eva smiled and nodded. Why waste another word, our meal was over, and we might never see her again. Joy and I confirmed our lunch date as she headed toward a table, and Randy and I headed out the back door leading to the parking lot.

Exiting the restaurant, the whiff of putrid air from the recently opened dumpster was apparent. It marked a sharp contrast to the scent of roasted and smoked meat that hung thick in the air of Balaton's.

"Thanks for lunch," I said to Randy as we both opened the doors of our cars. "My treat next time."

"You bet!" Randy was seated, had started his car, and was driving off while I was still settling into my seat and securely positioning my purse on the passenger side. Snapping the seatbelt into its holder, I checked the rearview window and caught sight of Joy coming out of the back door of Balaton's. As I watched, she jumped into the passenger side of a black Chevy, quickly embracing someone who most likely was a long-time business associate of her father, or from the size of his back, could have been an NFL lineman. As I pulled the car out, I made a mental note to call her and reinforce that I would and could not take her sister Rachel as a patient.

CHAPTER 5B

"Hey, Sister Nun, how was your reunion?" I could tell Kathy was distracted. She is not a particularly good driver even when she isn't on the phone. She believes she has great driving skills but claims it's just directions that mess up her driving. "Sister Nun, the reunion? You went didn't you?" Either we needed to go for a two-for-one deal with the hearing aids we were getting for Mom, or I needed to get her some Ginkgo Biloba memory herbs.

"Oh, yeah. I went." Now she remembers. "It was much better than I ever expected. The committee put a lot of work into making it a nice affair. I even recognized most of the girls and got to hook back up with Joyce Tucker. Remember her? Her nun name was Sr. Joy Marie."

"You mean the nun with the gutter mouth is still there? She used to freak me out going around cursing. Her parents had that big ass house on the lake and didn't her sister marry some black man just to piss off her Archie Bunker father?"

"Yep, that was Joy." Joy's personality was hard to forget

and her life circumstances easy to remember. “It was hard for me to believe that she was still there as well, but she is pretty radical in many ways. She’s gone rogue on the anything traditionally Catholic and spends her time with spirituality groups on Sundays who do things like drumming and hugging trees.”

“You’re kidding me.”

“Well, maybe not the hugging trees part, but she did tell me about the drumming community she attends on Sundays. We’ve had lunch a couple of times since the reunion. She hasn’t changed a bit.”

“That’s good. She was pretty cool for a nun and was never really wrapped up with nun-like thinking. You and Randy would have those lame conversations about the state of black America and the marginalization of black Catholics. Oh my God, when I think of Randy. What a waste of a good-looking man. What a waste. You know, you bringing up that nun is so funny. Not funny ha ha, but funny weird. I was just thinking about Joy the other day. I couldn’t remember her real name but that white chick that I was telling you about that showed up at Don’s funeral sorta looked like her. You know Don’s first wife was white and he only dated white women for a long time. I really think Jess might have been the only black woman that Don ever dated.”

“How is Jess doing? I need to give her a call.”

“She would appreciate that. Every passing week is a good thing. No news is good news as they say, but it’s still unsettling that the case isn’t closed. She’s taking one day at a time.”

"Listen, give Jess my love and tell her I will call her soon. I've got to go…just pulled up to the restaurant so we'll talk later."

The design proposal template on the computer screen begged to be completed for the two new clients that came in this week. Developing the design plan was much more enticing than preparing invoices that were way past due. These clients actually owed me money. Shucks, the plan to distract myself with a long conversation with Kath was thwarted. Damn her being busy. With the way business had picked up lately, I could no longer depend on Melody to send out invoices. I guess it was fair that her weekends were her weekends. Your kids don't always appreciate trying to keep all the money in the family anyway; so I might as well get a real business manager. One that didn't throw a temper tantrum when I told her she'd made a mistake. Lordy, lordy, that girl was sensitive. And Lord knows I didn't need any more drama in my life. I was on full-time drama duty with Jess.

Zipping open the canvas envelope with all the client receipts, I began to punch numbers on the calculator, a mindless but somewhat rewarding task. Listening to the rhythm of the clicking and watching numbers get bigger and bigger was somewhat relaxing. You would think I had money like Joy Tucker's family the way I let these invoices pile up. Sr. Joy

Marie. That is something that Kathy should bring her up, just when … damn, I lost track of … wait. Could that have been Joy at the funeral?

Immediately, the Word template on my computer was replaced with the Google screen. I quickly typed in Sr. Joyce Marie Tucker, Cleveland. The list ran long, beginning with St. Bede's Hospital. Two clicks later, her picture was visible.

"It's her. Or someone that could be her twin." I whispered into the screen while hitting the speed dial button for Jessica's number on the phone.

"Jess, do you remember the name of that family that Don claimed had invested in his fake video game business?"

I could hear her exasperation through the wire and didn't care about all the drama this inquiry was going to stir up.

CHAPTER 6

Connie Sims, the office manager of Psychological Health Care, Inc., never missed an opportunity to give me advice. No doubt, it was generally well warranted, generally appreciated, and always on point. Today was no exception.

"What makes you think reading about yoga will help you decide whether or not you should take a class? Why don't you just pay the fifteen bucks and take the darn class? That's one hour compared to years of studying the subject to see if you are ready or not."

"It wouldn't be years." I chuckled.

"No, really, if there was a PhD in yoga, you would feel you had to get it before you took a class." Connie was the queen of multitasking and didn't miss a step of adding electronic signatures of the various therapists to the insurance forms. Her eyes darted to the front entrance, and mine followed her direction to notice Joy Tucker walking through the door followed by her slightly younger and modern clone Rachel.

"Kathy, I'm glad I caught you." My surprise was noticeable and Joy responded in explanation. "I wanted you to see Rachel. I've been talking so much about you since the reunion, and I encouraged her to come and get an appointment, just as you suggested." Joy pulled me in a quick embrace that further cut off my breathing, which was already momentarily interrupted by Joy's assertion that I had agreed to see Rachel. "Please, help her. I owe you big time," she whispered as she released me from her embrace.

"Uh . . . Joy," I groped for words to forge my way out of this ambush, looking to Connie who shook her head back and forth to let me know I was on my own with this one. Rachel, whose auburn hair resembled Joy's with the benefit of pricey salon highlights, swung the side ponytail back over her shoulder and followed Joy in giving me a hug.

"You look so much younger out of that creepy ole' habit." Rachel giggled. The pitch and tone of Rachel's voice resembled more of an adolescent girl than an almost forty-year-old adult. "I would have recognized you anywhere, even though I haven't seen you since the time when Jamal and I wanted to get married and Joy brought you into that big, cold auditorium where we used to sit and visit her to remind Dad that he could really be okay with black people and that they even did good things like become nuns." Rachel paused, reflecting on her own words.

"Oh, geez. I didn't mean that in a bad way." Rachel noticed the puzzled look on my face that was born out the connection

I had just made to Jamal being her husband. She had linked my perplexity to the reference of her father's racism. Without knowing Jamal's last name, I could only assume it was the same Jamal who was now in Randy's counsel. Didn't Randy say Jamal was not only grieving his friend's death, but that his marriage was failing? With this realization, I was suddenly traveling with Alice down some rabbit hole, except that we weren't headed to Wonderland.

"Would you like to move into Dr. Carpenter's office?" Connie suggested, seeing that this conversation was going to lead to more than the usual good to see you remarks and into a conversation she really didn't want to hear. "You have just about twenty minutes, Dr. Carpenter, before your next appointment," Connie instructed us, gratefully providing an end point to the ambush.

"I've got to run and meet one of the physician liaisons across town. My mission is accomplished connecting the two of you." Joy nodded to Connie, tapped the front desk, and quickly exited the front door.

"What?" Connie responded to the question that I had not asked. "She just called yesterday to see when your schedule was open." The suspicious origin of the floral spray that had been delivered moments before they arrived was now apparent. Connie smiled and shrugged her shoulders as I made the connection, as if to say don't blame me for accepting a good bribe from a nun. She continued her work, allowing Rachel and I to get introduced to what looked like might become a new relationship as therapist and patient.

"Joy was on me like white on rice to get some help, and I kept telling her I wasn't going to just pick up the phone book or maybe not a phone book, 'cause you don't use those big fat yellow pages these days, but maybe go online and Google 'therapist' and pick one and just spill out everything that I have been holding in for twenty years." The thirty-second walk to my corner office on the east end of the refurbished century home now seemed to be taking at least an hour with Rachel's chattering. "Then Joy remembered that you were some famous therapist. Actually she didn't remember until she had to come to the house one day because I was frea... king out, I mean really freaking out, that even Joy, who could walk around the Flats downtown unarmed at one in the morning and dare someone to attack her, was scared that I would off myself or something. She had to stay home with me the next day..."

We had entered the office, and I motioned for Rachel to take a seat. She needed no encouragement to continue talking. This was a woman who gave new meaning to the word loquacious. "... She wanted to make sure that I really didn't off myself, and I knew that I must have been pretty bad because usually Joy gets on my damn nerves worse than any parent, even our own, but that day I was so happy that she was with me and we just sat all day watching TV. Joy had never seen all the morning shows... not even Oprah when she was on, even though she came on here at four o'clock, but in Atlanta she was on in the morning and in the evening... anyway, you happened to be on *Morning Exchange*, and Joy got real excited 'cause you and her used to be so close when you were a nun, and she hadn't seen you in so long, and she didn't even realize that you were such a famous shrink. I guess she knew that you were a shrink. I'm sorry, Sister, I mean psychiatrist." Rachel threw her head back and laughed. "I called you Sister, so sorry." The laugh was the edgewise I needed to get a word in.

"Rachel," I urged. "Let's talk about expectations for a minute. We only have a few minutes left, so I would like to talk about the psychologist-therapist relationship and what we might be able to do together to help you."

"Sure. Sure." Rachel straightened her back against the beige leather swivel chair as if she forgot that she had been called to the principal's office for talking too much during class. I still was not clear whether or not I would or could actually put Rachel on my caseload, and if this chatter was indicative of what a typical session was like, I was heavily leaning toward making a referral. In the time it took me to think referral, Rachel had burst into tears, gasping for breath in intervals between sounds resembling nail scratching on a chalkboard.

"Rachel, tell me what the tears are about?" Like a soap opera actress, Rachel's emotional shift was only partially convincing and somewhat disingenuous. And like a soap opera actress, she eerily seemed to become even more beautiful as she deescalated.

"Living without him is much worse than I ever imagined it would be. I don't know if I can go on without him in my life." The wailing began again.

"Are you referring to Jamal? Do we need to make the sessions couples' counseling?

Rachel's wail instantly turned into laughter. Oh, gosh, I was dealing with Sybil and all her multiple personalities.

"It would be easy to go on without Jamal, he's really married to the business; although it would complicate things financially, and money's important to me. I've got to stay in the lifestyle I'm accustomed to, but needing Jamal is not in the same way I needed Don." The tears began to flow in nice lines without even a smear to her foundation.

She swallowed and said, "Don Davenport was the love of my life."

"Don Davenport?" I questioned and Rachel nodded while continuing to cry.

The three short rings from the phone and caller identification of the source as the front desk signaled my next patient was waiting. It was my turn to wail.

CHAPTER 7

"You would have to understand that sometimes a marriage isn't about love. Wasn't that the point Beyoncé made in that song? Or maybe it was Tina Turner? Yeah it was the older one, 'cause I remember I sang it to my first real love when I broke up with him and I was in junior high. He didn't get what I was trying to say, either." Rachel sensed that I was just not buying her defense of marriage spiel, especially one where she claimed an outside love interest somehow stabilized her marriage to Jamal. We were not progressing very fast in the therapeutic process. The last two sessions were used as a sanctum for actively grieving Don's death; after all, as she told me, she was practically his wife.

It also didn't help that she was consistently late. Her arrival ten minutes into the scheduled time was now a pattern. Upon arrival today, she shamelessly showcased her new purchase as the reason for her tardiness. Her further explanation: one would think that it wouldn't take a sales clerk fifteen minutes to finalize a sale especially after she had spent over an hour deciding on which Badgley Mischka bag best fit her physique. A seasoned clerk would have anticipated a purchase and had her out of the store in time for her appointment within minutes of her decision. She positioned the bag against her thigh and over her shoulder as I imagined which outfit in *my* closet would match the red leather purse with gold zippers. It was minutes before I remembered this was a patient that I needed to provide treatment for rather than treat her like a girlfriend coming over for lunch. I quickly got a grip and requested that we focus on another of Rachel's favorite topics, herself.

"Don't get me wrong, Jamal and I work well together. We always have." Rachel glanced down at her purse as if it were a small puppy seated next to her. "From the very beginning, our relationship has always been kind of an arrangement anyway. Daddy was like our business manager. You know, like those movie stars with the fake marriages." Soft waves of hair fell backward hitting her shoulder as she laughed. "What is up with me today? It's not only movie stars who have fake marriages but basketball and football players do too. And they all have a bunch of lawyers just to defend their little secrets. But people know because they are fooling around with somebody and those some bodies talk. Anyway, Jamal is just as much eye candy as any of those movie stars even after all of these years. And come to think of it, Jamal's a little gay too."

"Okay, I am trying to connect the dots here. Your marriage works because it's fake and your father arranged it and because Jamal is gay?" The questions expressed aloud were companions to the ones that were on my mind. Hadn't Tina's painter claimed that Jamal was on the down-low? Was Joy's disclosure about her father's "investment" in Rachel's marriage during casual lunch conversation intentional? Did she want me to have this information to understand how to treat her better or was there something more to this investment?

"Maybe both," Rachel was uncharacteristically pensive. "I think Jamal is one of those metrosexual guys who appreciate gay men for their style and confidence. You know, you grow into that kind of attitude in Atlanta just because. Just because..." She paused and whispered. "You know there are so many of them in Atlanta. Not that there's anything wrong with it." Rachel laughed. "You remember that *Seinfeld* episode? 'Not that there's anything wrong with it.'" She looked at me quizzing, "You didn't watch *Seinfeld*?"

Every mental tracking tool that I had learned in graduate school was taxed during a session with Rachel. "Yes, I watched *Seinfeld* and I remember the episode and you are saying that your husband is not gay, but just appreciates gay men. What about the business arrangement with your father?"

"That's funny. They say black people didn't watch *Seinfeld*. Jamal used to say that and said I probably liked it because I was white and all white people love *Seinfeld*. I saw every episode, some of them two or three times. That would be funny—if you liked *Seinfeld* and your husband didn't. Joy told me you were married to a white guy, just the opposite of Jamal and me." Rachel's posture straightened as she caught my look that screamed at her to focus. "Uh, yeah…Jamal isn't gay. You think I would know. I'm his wife. Although that woman who was married to the governor, McGreevey, claimed she didn't know. At least that's what she said on *Oprah* or maybe it was *The View*? But she was just saving face because what is she going to say? 'Yes, I knew he was gay, and I just let him have all of his boy toys.'" This time my focus command face didn't work. Rachel was suddenly caught up experiencing a moment when the lights just got turned on. "Oh, my gosh! Do you think I might be like that governor's wife?"

This session was like an egg without a shell. A gooey mess. I took a deep breath and dove in. "Rachel, that might be a question worth exploring later, but a priority for now is to lay out the current state of your marriage and determine what might need changing." Rachel appeared to be disinterested and instantly bored in that direction and began shifting in her chair like a toddler at a very long church service. You had to love Rachel's charm, but it also proved to be exhausting.

"Our time is up for today. Are you interested in rescheduling?" I was relieved the session was over, and the question was really a standard intake question typically asked after the first several sessions as confirmation of commitment to the process, but Rachel took it personally.

"You don't want to keep seeing me? Did I do something wrong? I'll get here on time from now on. Joy will kill me if I don't keep coming. She's already threatened to limit the funds from the inheritance if I don't get my act together. Jamal and

I need to work this out 'cause at this age, I can't start a career, gee, I couldn't even get a job, let alone a career. I only know how to spend money, not make money. And what would that mean for Trenton. Oh, God, I have got to get over Don but how do you act like someone didn't matter to you when you were in love with him and he's the father of your son." On cue, Rachel tears appeared.

"Excuse me?"

"Oh, shoot. I thought you knew that from back in your nun days when Joy brought you to visiting sessions to convince Daddy that it was okay for me to marry Don, and Daddy making my life into a business deal decided it was better to marry the good Negro, Jamal. I thought you might have even given him the idea and recommended that I hook up with somebody more appropriate for me to marry."

Hoping to ease the headache that had instantly erupted, I began vigorously rubbing my forehead. "I'm not following you at all. I am very confused."

"Never mind," she quickly responded. "I'll fill in the details next time. I'm already late for my nail appointment. You'll remind me, okay, that Trenton's daddy is where we left off." Rachel reached into the newly purchased Badgley Mischka bag and pulled out a compact, patting her tear lines with powder. "Woo, that was a rough session," she declared.

CHAPTER 8

"Hey, I called out three times and you didn't respond," Jon reacted in defense of causing my startle response when he wrapped his arms around my shoulders. "What's in the mail that's got you so engrossed?"

The grocery store circulars, donation request letter from the American Cancer Society, and an insurance explanation of benefits notice received absent-minded attention as my full attention was still attached to my session with Rachel.

"Sorry. It's nothing in the mail, just still decomposing work I guess." I gave him a soft peck on the check and tossed the mail on the counter.

"I thought you might have seen the invitation from Sr. Joy to the children's hospital benefit. Chicken dinners are costing a lot these days." Jon picked up an overripe apple from the fruit basket on the counter, tossed it in the air, and took a bite out of its soft side. It brought a quick smile to my face as he spit it out and then rotated it to its peak side. "Tickets are six hundred dollars a person, but considering medical costs, it makes sense."

"I didn't see it, but she asked me about it when we had lunch last week." Connecting with Joy over the last several months since the reunion was costing some money, to say nothing of her sister Rachel challenging my professional sensibilities. Yet, the comfort of connecting again with someone who shared your past and the easy laughter and silent tears that resulted from that connection overrode the donation requests. I was happy to support Joy's ministry even if she didn't label it as such and working with Rachel unfortunately, came with the territory.

Jon scanned the inside of the nearly empty refrigerator for something that might be put together for a meal. It was my second apology for the evening, and I had only been home ten minutes.

"Sorry, honey. I know it's my turn, and I said I would go shopping this week. I meant to pick up something on my way home but got distracted. How about if I order a pizza or better yet we can go over to Arturo's? It shouldn't be too crowded."

Within an hour we were seated in the leather-cushioned booth and had placed an order for what we considered to be the best Italian food in Little Italy in an area that boasted the best Italian restaurants in the Midwest. The family atmosphere, the friendly patrons, and the wit of the owner who routinely made the rounds welcoming newcomers and visiting regulars like Jon and me made you appreciate an ordinary day. It also made you love the fact that life was best when it was just okay. No fireworks needed.

Jon and I sat in a comfortable silence waiting for the shrimp pesto pizza to be brought to our table, when Joy's voice filled the booth.

"Are you guys stalking me?"

The swallow of wine almost went down the wrong pipe as I looked up to witness Joy's sly smile.

"I would say it's the other way around," I managed to voice my response. Jon stood up and gave Joy a hug and gestured for her to join us as I scooted over in the booth.

"Thanks, but actually I can't stay. I just stopped in for happy hour and met one of Dad's attorneys to wrap up some business and I'm on my way out."

"We've ordered the shrimp pizza, so have a slice before you go. It will only take a few minutes, and you probably need to eat dinner." I prodded.

"No need to ask twice." Joy quickly positioned herself just in time for the server to place the large pizza on the pedestal platter.

"Y'all better order another one for I can down half of this one before you get to a second slice." We were quickly engaged in a spirited conversation of Cleveland politics, Mayor Marvan's appointment to school superintendent of his best friend, Patrick Simpson, and a former Clevelander, Tiara Jones, who was recently fired from *The Real Housewives of Atlanta* for being dirt poor and lacking the creativity to come up with a story line where she could have even faked being rich.

“I can’t believe you actually watch that show,” I said. “How do you find the time?” Joy had shared the news of Tiara’s firing with the same priority ranking as she shared the recent change in reimbursement from the health insurance company that would affect the bottom line of the hospital she managed.

“Actually Rachel started me watching that crazy show, and believe me it is easier to watch it on TV versus seeing the same drama that’s on the show happening before my very own eyes with her life. I mean Jamal is a great guy… a little too wrapped up in work, but even his patience will run out with Rachel’s shenanigans.” She paused to swallow. “Kathy, I thought you were supposed to have her put together by now?” Joy teased and I smiled but didn’t dare take the bait. “Really, does she need to come twice a week? I’ll pay you three times your rate if you can knock the crazy out of her faster,” Joy laughed and continued. “I’m serious. It’s all Dad’s money anyway, and you can be damn sure I’m taking it out of Rachel’s share since she’s not getting a penny of her haul until she gets her life together.”

“Oh, gee, no pressure here.” I turned to Jon and smirked.

“Hey, I’m not in this conversation, but if I were…” Jon teasingly paused, “… I would say something like I find it interesting that you’ve got some kind of trust fund for an almost forty-year-old woman.”

"Not my terms. It's Dad still ruling from the grave. There were conditions under which each of us would get our inheritance. Rachel needs to stay married to Jamal as long as he is employed at Ubold, the grocery retail holding company that Dad founded. If anything, Dad knew a good business man when he saw one, no matter what color skin he had. Jamal was always being wooed to competitors, and inheriting a fifteen billion dollar business was a great incentive for him to stay. And get this one: I need to stay in the convent and set up a foundation that can be managed only by me." Joy gave a sarcastic chuckle. "Even in his death, he would be embarrassed if I left the convent. He used the fact that he had a daughter that was a nun as his cover for being a good Christian, which, by the way, helps in building a company brand and also in the political world where he was a shadow powerhouse behind a number of US congressmen who owed more than their careers to him. Poor Dad probably thought I was his ticket to heaven, and if I left he would find himself on a fast slide to hell. Little did he know, I am probably following him there."

"I doubt that," I quickly said, noting how convinced Joy seemed that both she and her father were condemned.

"Those are some pretty clear terms with an obvious message for you and Rachel." Jon stated.

"He only had one message his entire life, and it was *I control you.*" Joy pointed to me and Jon emphasizing the meaning of her words. "Dad always wanted a son and he got me and Rachel. He then tried to settle for a son-in-law whom he could treat like a son. I ended up marrying Christ," she gestured air quotes when she said "marrying Christ," "and Rachel ended up bringing home black guys. My card-carrying John Birch Society father had a rough time with that one. How could he end up without a son and then be faced with a black son-in-law? In the end, his rational self took over, and he reasoned if his only grandkids were going to be half–black, then at least he had to control which black guy it would be and influence what the black guy did for a living. All of this is still part of his plan. He's still controlling us from the grave."

Comments that Rachel had just made a few hours ago in the session were floating in my mind when we were simultaneously interrupted by the server soliciting dessert orders and my phone buzzer indicating a text message. Impulsively opening the app, I recognized Tina's number and placed the phone back in the purse pocket deciding to read the message and call her later. Still, a peculiar energy remained and nudged my spirit back to the message. I intuitively picked the phone back up and began to read the text.

"Oh, my God!" I screamed, catching the attention of several patrons in the nearby booth. "Jessica's been arrested," I announced to Jon and Joy with curious diners benefiting from what would quickly be a hot news item not only in Atlanta but in Cleveland.

CHAPTER 9

Every bone in my body felt the pain of being disconnected and defenseless. Ten long hours behind bars left Jessica comatose and sent Tina into histrionic fits. When it came to managing personal crises, especially those that involved family, I was wilted spinach. Jon was masterfully handling every aspect of Jessica's defense—from securing the best criminal attorney in Atlanta through a contact of a frat buddy—to negotiating paid time off from the television station while she awaited the decision of a grand jury. The meantime strategy was for Tina to stay glued to Jess 24/7, and for her agent to manage the public relations nightmare this had created for Atlanta's media darling. I was tasked with praying.

The ritual of the liturgy was the perfect backdrop for laying down worries. Randy's voice, as he recited the introductory rite, layered over my reverberating thoughts, which helped my mind to extract what semblance of peace it could find. There was just the voice and the ritual: The familiar ritual of grade school First Fridays; the ritual I attended with the white dress, veil, and white tights and received Communion for the first time; the ritual that captured my commitment to religious life; the same ritual that later joined Jon and me in marriage; the ritual that celebrated the life of my father before we tearfully laid him to his final resting place; the ritual that allowed me to face the every days when I didn't feel the strength needed to navigate the hours.

"You were in deep meditation this morning. You didn't even crack a smile at my joke." Randy walked the few steps from the small chapel where daily Mass was held to his parish office across the hall. Our morning check-ins had become as much a part of the ritual as the liturgy.

"You made a joke?" I said. Randy did indeed have a sense of humor which I thoroughly enjoyed and was instantly disappointed that I missed an opportunity to have it influence my mood.

"I do occasionally use humor to get a point across, but it's falling flat these days."

"I'm sorry. Just a bit preoccupied with what's going on with Jessica."

"I know. And I am sorry about all that. Jess's a great gal and doesn't deserve all of this drama. Jamal has called me at least three times really, really angry that they have gone after her."

"That makes at least three of us. Tina is beyond crazy and uncharacteristically worried that this will not blow over easily which is what's got me so off-centered. It's all a bad nightmare."

"Well, Jamal's pretty confident that's it just a matter of time before she's cleared. He claims there are too many other shady characters to go after, and the police were just trying to draw some attention to the case. It will be okay, Kath. It will be okay." He looked at me compassionately, knowing that our anxiety would not be diminished until Jessica was no longer considered a suspect.

"Well, it's funny that they consider Jessica to be one of the shady characters. If he knows them, why doesn't he just direct the police's attention on whom they could concentrate?" The sarcasm oozing out of my mouth, to my surprise, landed on its intended source.

"Hey, Fr. Randy," Jamal called as he stepped out of the driver's side of the Cadillac sedan that was possibly a rental car, "I was trying to make it in for Mass and I'm glad that I caught you." Jamal approached and extended his hand to me, "Sorry to interrupt, Doctor. I'm Jamal Nelson, Rachel's husband."

"Yes, we met at Randy's ordination anniversary party." I studied his facial features as if he were a national monument, hoping that he had not heard my comment. There was something so engaging about Jamal's total appearance. I had not connected him with Rachel at the time of the ordination, but as a couple, the two certainly exuded Hollywood quality.

Randy embraced Jamal, lightly pounding him on the

back. "You didn't say you would be in town again so soon when we talked."

"Unplanned trip to bring my son who wanted to see his mom. Rachel's not very communicative on the phone so I thought we could both check in on her." Jamal's penetrating look seemed to beg for information, or maybe my discomfort from being in the presence of the husband of my patient and the brother-in-law of a good friend was freaking me out. "Rachel tells me you're really helping her." I averted Jamal's soft eyes of gratitude.

"Sure, no problem. Thanks." I turned directly to Randy. "Randy, got to go. Talk with you later."

"I really didn't mean to interrupt. I can come back, Father, after I head downtown for a meeting." Jamal quickly glanced at me then at Randy.

"No, really," I said, already having walked the hundred feet to open my SUV's door. "I've got to run." Quickly pulling the seat belt over my shoulder and securing the buckle, I felt peculiarly tied down in more ways that I cared to imagine. There was something disconcerting about Jamal's presence that was not connected to the initial discomfort of meeting someone with alarmingly good looks.

Connie's smirk when I came through the front door alerted me that something was up. "Good morning," she said and with a nod of the head directed my attention to the waiting area where Rachel sat with a young male whose body's muscular tone was that of a personal trainer or managed by one. His hair appeared to have natural highlights or had the attention of a highly paid stylist. He turned and gave me a celebrity smile, sounding whistles on my gaydar. Rachel jumped up from her chair.

"Sister, I mean Dr. Kathy. This is my son, Trenton. I thought you wouldn't mind if I brought him to my session today, especially since, you know, we were going to talk about his origins." Was Rachel actually winking at me? "His dad…I mean Jamal," she looked at me and winked again, "just brought him to see me last night for a few days so I didn't want to let him out of my sight today. I couldn't believe he actually was here. You know how these young guys are, and he has a lot going on in his life with school and his music. I didn't tell you he's got the best singing voice. I don't know who he got it from 'cause certainly I can't hit a decent note and Jamal…well, maybe…anyway, he's going to try out for *American Idol* or *The Voice*. They say *The Voice* is better these days so maybe you'll want to put your energy auditioning for that show." She gave a loving expression to her son who happened to share the same demeanor as Jamal.

"Mom…" Trenton displayed a shy look reminiscent of what I had just witnessed with Jamal or maybe that was an imagined resemblance. I scanned his face for phenotype resemblance. His beige-tone-colored complexion and wavy straight hair and fuller lips were characteristically biracial.

"Excuse me while I go to my office." I turned to the front desk to see Connie hiding her laughter and shaking her head. "If you don't mind, I need to get settled. I will be out at nine to get you, or Connie can just bring you back." Arriving a half hour early, Rachel had kept her commitment to coming on time for the next session but maintained her unpredictability by bringing her son. "I'm sure you two can keep each other busy while I get ready for our session."

Rachel's file, along with those of the other patients for the day, lay on top of the neat pile on my desk. I picked it up along with the mug of chamomile tea that Connie had graciously handed me as I walked down the hall.

"I put a shot of vodka in it. You are going to need it," she teased.

The hot liquid sizzled down my throat making me wonder if Connie had actually put a shot in there, or if the anticipated conversation with Rachel was getting me fired up. A typical treatment plan was useless with Rachel. It was more like go with the flow and work to keep her focused on the goal that had yet to be determined other than for her to get her life together. Did that mean getting her back to Atlanta for more shopping? Did it matter who Trenton's biological father was, if she needed to remain married to Jamal to secure her lifestyle? And if Don Davenport was his biological father, then what good would it do to for that to be public knowledge at this point?

The case notes resembled an adolescent girl's diary with all the recorded accounts of Rachel's tears of her real or imagined love for a man who was now dead. Here I was counseling Rachel over the loss while Randy worked with...oh, my God, Jamal? Did Jamal know that his wife was in love with his friend? Or if Jamal was on the down-low, was he involved with Don? Is that why Jessica finally ended the relationship? She could compete with another woman but not with a man? Geez. Oh, doo doo balls. I don't want to know all of this especially with Jessica being accused of... The pages from Rachel's file fell to the floor as the ringing phone brought me back to reality.

"Do you want me to send them back? Or do you need more time? It's after nine." Connie's voice instantly grounded me. "Hey, and by the way, I knew nothing about her bringing pretty boy or I would have given you a heads up."

"That's okay. I'm sorry. I just lost track of time. Please send them back."

Seconds later, Rachel entered giggling as Trenton whispered something in her ear.

"Boy, you ought to quit saying stuff like that." Rachel tapped her son on the shoulder showcasing the platinum band ring of diamonds on her left hand. "Dr. K, Trenton says you don't look like a nun who wouldn't have got none."

"Mom!" Trenton gently chastised her, obviously proud of

himself for his ingenuity and for what I knew to be the most unoriginal nun joke around.

"You can have a seat here." I smiled and motioned to Trenton to take the adjacent bucket leather swivel chair rather than sit on the arm of the one where his mother sat. He obediently did so, acting as if I had broken up a classroom seating arrangement with his girlfriend.

"I hope it's okay that I had Trenton come with me." The statement was not made for my benefit. Rachel smiled lovingly at her son, and obviously she had no intention of asking permission for his presence. "It was just so convenient because we were just getting ready to talk about you anyway." Rachel found this amusing and paused for a few seconds to laugh. "Actually, we were going to talk about your daddy." Nonplussed, Trenton's gaze remained fixed on his mother. She remained enamored with his presence which gave me a moment to jump in before her motor mouth revved up.

"Rachel, before you go there, if I could hear from Trenton how he feels about being here and I would like for us to have some clear boundaries for what we want to put out in the session today."

"Oh, Trenton knows all the stuff I have to say. He's really my best friend. You know, with Jamal working all the time when he was growing up and all, he and I did everything together. My little man even was my date to some of the community events I had to attend when Jamal was out of town. After all, what would it look like if I brought another male as my escort; people would really start to talk and then Jamal would get so jealous. Not really jealous of anybody else with me, but more embarrassed. That's it. He would get embarrassed. You know he was just like Daddy in that respect—you had to keep up the image for the company more so than the family. Anyway, my Trenton here actually didn't mind. You loved going with Mommy. Do you remember fashion week and all the shows we saw? Once we snuck into a Cavalli show because that lying Kim told me she would have tickets for us and she didn't, but Trenton was able to distract the ticket taker with his cute little self..."

"Rachel, thanks for sharing," I intentionally interrupted. "I am glad you enjoy your son's company." Rachel sat erect, a position that somehow helped her to get into adult mode. "Trenton, are you okay with being here? You always have the option of waiting for your mom outside, or actually, if you want to have a few minutes with me alone if you need to say anything privately, that's okay too." Trenton eyes popped a bit at the mention of having private time.

"Uh, it's okay. I'm used to my mom." He was surprisingly sheepish when on center stage.

"That's good, and if anytime during the session you feel uncomfortable with what surfaces, please know that you can change your mind. Just let me know." Trenton returned my smile, and I knew we had connected. Rachel's silence was off–putting, since in the month that I had worked with her,

I rarely had the opportunity to drive the conversation. I did not hesitate to take the lead.

"Let's start at the end point. And by that I mean, what would you like to see different about your life as a family right now?" I hoped that would put us in forward direction versus triggering Rachel to go down memory lane about the other possible Trenton daddies, but it only set off a sea of tears.

"I don't know what I imagined for my family to be, but I never imagined the life I have now. Sorry, baby..." she looked at Trenton, grabbed a tissue, and blew her nose in a seamless motion, "...you are my heart, but you've grown up and want your own friends. I can't be one of your college buddies. I know that." Trenton immediately moved to the arm of the chair where his mother sat and began rubbing her back. "I just thought the magic in my life would continue. I know that's naïve, but when Jamal and I were first together he used to be a lot of fun, kicking it all the time, but then Daddy must have drugged him to be his clone 'cause he got all wrapped up in that damn business. I know it pays the bills and keeps me in this lifestyle, but there is no fun, no fun, just no fun. When Don was around, at least it was fun. It was like being back in the day..." Trenton's direct eye contact commanded me to intervene.

"Rachel, your happiness seems to be so connected to Don. Help me out here. Explain his relationship to your family." Luckily, Trenton's voice became prominent.

"He and Dad go way back, so he was like my uncle. Mom really liked him and wished sometimes she could have married him instead of Dad, although she barely knew him growing up." Trenton had an uncanny knack for normalizing crazy.

"Only because Daddy had me in that boarding school and I didn't get to hang out with all the Cleveland kids. Everyone, though, knew Don." She turned and stared directly at me as if she wanted me to confirm this for Trenton. "You remember he was a teenage star, at least in Cleveland. He had that part in the one of the early TV shows that they filmed in Cleveland, like the Nickelodeon." She paused and blew her nose hard into a tissue. "And he even danced on *Upbeat*, you remember, Cleveland's version of *American Bandstand*. Cleveland had its own version of all the national shows." I remembered *Upbeat* and the host Don Webster, but certainly did not know that Don Davenport was one of the few blacks who would have been featured on that show when it aired. I would have already been a novice in the convent at that time and certainly not watching popular variety shows.

"Don was destined to be a star and would have been if his family hadn't derailed him," Rachel sighed and began to cry again. "He ended up being my star. Without him I didn't have a life. He gave me back my life."

Trenton again looked at me as if I had a magic wand that could change the course of her destiny in an instant. "When Grandpa died, Mom told me that she was now free to be in the relationship that she was meant to be in. It was kinda' weird, but that's when she started talking about Uncle Don like he was my dad."

"He could be your dad. Grandpa broke us up when I got pregnant and made me marry your father." Trenton again looked at me.

"Were you aware of this?" He didn't appear to be hearing this for the first time.

"It is what she says, but Auntie Joyce says it is not true. She says Mom was pretty rebellious and only dated Don once, more like a blind date for a dance at the boarding school, and she did that to get back at Dad. Grandpa did try to break up Mom and Dad when they were dating, but Mom has always been and still is, crazy for Dad. I mean that literally." Trenton smiled and Rachel grunted and I decided to let us all sit with this analysis. Thank God for her silence, however eerie it made me feel. Trenton's information was proving far more useful for therapeutic progress. I stayed focused on him.

"What do you think? And, more importantly, how is all of this affecting you?"

"I think Mom's just going through a lot. She's been pretty lonely since I left for school, and then Grandpa died, then Uncle Don." His beautiful face was crestfallen.

"And what about you?"

"Grandpa was cool with me, although as I got older, I knew he was disappointed that I wasn't into sports as much as he was, and he didn't like the direction my life was headed because it certainly would not be Ubold. Even with all that, Grandpa is hard to miss because he wasn't around even when he was there, if you know what I mean," he paused reflectively.

"I miss Uncle Don, though." Struggling not to cry he continued, "He was helping me sort out some personal stuff, but Dad's cool with all of it now, and in a strange way, Uncle Don's dying brought Dad and me closer."

"Personal stuff?" I caught Rachel's face and for the first time experienced a hint of anger.

"Yeah, for a while there I thought Uncle Don just might be my father because he accepted pretty easily that I'm gay. But, I know for sure that my dad is my dad." He pounded his right fist into his open left palm.

"You can't know that for sure. I don't know that for sure and I'm your mother. I would know who I slept with at the time," Rachel defiantly said, suddenly looking all of her forty years. I wondered if she had any inkling that this was the direction the session would take.

Trenton knelt in front of his mother's chair, his pant legs touching her knees. "Mom, trust me. I have proof. I know that you wish it weren't true, but even if you left Dad for what you believed to be the family that was meant to be, Uncle Don wasn't going to be with you and he is not my biological father." He looked up at Rachel. "I'm sorry to be so blunt, Mom. I want you to get better and come home. Dad wants you to get better and come home. We just want to get all of this in the past."

"That's just it. Once *this* is all in the past, what do I have left?" Rachel was pathetically poignant in nailing her predicament. Her therapy was just about to begin.

CHAPTER 10

"Hey, I hear the session with Rachel and the Tucker family saga is adding a lot of drama to your therapy practice." Joy sliced through the largest cut of cowboy rib eye that I had ever seen at Ruth Chris Steakhouse. With Jon out of town for a conference and a mutual Wednesday open without evening appointments, we treated ourselves to a leisurely dinner.

"Joy, you know I'm not going to talk about my sessions with Rachel and you shouldn't be bringing it up. Besides, I want to get your opinion on the Vatican's increased oversight on nuns for not promoting church teaching and taking positions opposite the bishops."

"You're kidding me, right? You want to talk about that, and you want to know what I think?" Joy gulped about an ounce of wine.

"Yes, I do. I'm not just trying to change the subject. I actually read the Doctrinal Assessment of the Leadership

Conference of Women Religious and I'm interested in your thoughts."

"And why the hell you would want to read that is beyond me. God, you're still more of a nun than I am. But you want my opinion? I have a few words in response to their assessment of 'radical feminism' and 'corporate dissent' and 'distorted vision.' They can kiss my religious ass. No, I change my mind. I don't want them to kiss my ass, because they would probably enjoy that..."

"Whoa!" I put up both hands, begging her to stop before lightning struck our booth. If she was trying to get me to change the topic back to Rachel's therapy, it worked. "You're right. The sessions with Rachel have been revealing, but we are finally doing some good work, and you are surely getting your money's worth, or your dad's money's worth."

Joy devilishly smiled. I didn't doubt she felt those sentiments toward the bishops, and I should have known full well that she knew I would be in agreement with what she was saying, but I definitely would have phrased it differently. The scary part is that Joy would say it just that way to any bishop. I prayed she would never have the opportunity. Do you get extra jail time for assaulting a bishop?

"We are getting our money's worth and then some. Seriously, I want to thank you. Rachel is the most reflective and appropriately responsive that I have known her to be in her life. You would have thought that bubble of having this dream life with Don Davenport would have been burst when he died. I'm glad you've got her focused on getting her marriage on track. It would help if the police could just relent with the investigation. How's your friend Jessica doing by the way?"

"As well as can be expected under the circumstances, I guess. They continue to dig and that remains disconcerting." I reached into the shared plate of asparagus and placed two stems on my saucer.

"It will be over soon." Joy said with confidence. "You can't get blood from a turnip, and they're going for blood."

"Yeah, but they can make a mountain out of a molehill and are scrutinizing every dime that went to him and requiring an explanation for every dollar." I made reference to what Tina had told me about the careful audit of Jessica's and Don's bank account.

"It is just a matter of time." Joy reiterated. "No foul, no play."

I laughed, "You're full of maxims this evening."

"It comes with age. God forbid, I am sounding like my father. Speaking of my father, I really hate to bring this up and have been waiting for a good time to even come near the topic. And before I ask, please know that on my own accord, this is not something I would ever ask of anyone, let alone a friend, so I won't blame you for feeling put upon. As you know, Dad liked to control things. One of the conditions for the release of inheritance funds is that Trenton gets some gay reversal therapy."

"Excuse me. Excuse me."

"Yes, you heard right, Kath."

"There is no such thing, Joy, and if there is such a therapy, it's being done by quacks and certainly no one I would or could give you a referral for."

"I'm not asking for a referral, Kathy. I was hoping you would see him."

"Oh, no, Joy. You can't be serious, and you've got to know where I stand…"

"I do know where you stand, which is exactly why I am asking that you be the one to see him. It just has to be for a few sessions, and then the attorneys require a brief report."

"What report—that says he's been cured? Joy, come on. I have done my part here with Rachel as a patient."

"Apparently Dad read some articles on reparative therapy on homosexual men and was convinced that it would work for Trenton, especially since he is only nineteen. He found a specialist in Atlanta who contacted Trenton several times. You can imagine how upsetting it was for him." Joy reached over and took my hand, noticing how upsetting this was for me just hearing this.

"Dad genuinely loved Trenton and wanted the best for him. He knew how cruel a world it would be for him as a black gay male." Joy paused, "Funny how being black didn't bother Dad anymore after he found out his only grandson was gay."

"Trenton appears to be a well-adjusted, grounded young man despite what his family has put him through." I said empathetically, hoping Mr. Tucker would hear me in whatever universe he now resided.

"Which is why it should be you that sees him and writes the report."

"Are you asking me to say that I did reparative therapy? I can't do that."

"But you can say you tried, and it didn't work. Dad's dead, Kath, but he got some attorneys whom he also controlled, so they are crossing every "t" and dotting every "i." Unfortunately it is a huge sum of money at stake, and all of the conditions have to be met before it's released. Trust me—the attorneys want their share as well, so they won't be scrutinizing the report very hard."

"I'm not licensed in Georgia." I made a feeble attempt at an excuse for not being able to do it.

"We can fly him here. His mom is still here so it is convenient, and the family home is in Ohio."

I thought about the alternative of Trenton actually having to go through such an experience and the damage it would do. In principle, that weighed heavier on me than saying I was conducting reversal therapy and not really doing it.

"They'll check my credentials and see that I do not claim this area as one of my competencies."

"Your credentials are impeccable, and they will assume that as a former nun and practicing Catholic that you are predisposed to this work."

"You have really thought this through, haven't you?" Joy

had calculated our renewal of friendship at the reunion to get me to see her sister and probably all along had planned for me to see Trenton as well. After all, she knew the provisions of her father's will long before the reunion. My stomach churned, and a sudden bout of acid reflux hit my throat.

"I'm so sorry. I know this looks like I'm using you in all of the worst possible ways." Joy was as astute as she was calculating. "There are few people that I actually trust in this world and you are the first on the list." I swallowed, wishing I had some antacid.

"I would understand if you said no and walked away. I am praying and hoping that you won't, but I would understand." Joy pleaded, "Someday I can share more about this. It will make much more sense. I just desperately need your support right now. Can I count on it?"

There was really no alternative. "I'll do it," I said before reason took over. Noticing Joy's smile, I quickly continued, "But with no guarantee that I write a report. If I find myself feeling too much out of my comfort zone and off-centered I will stop."

"Understood. I could not and would not ask for more." The strength of Joy's clutch over my hand was noticeably reassuring.

CHAPTER 11

Trenton arrived on time and well prepared for each session. Unlike his mother his focus was razor sharp, sharing details in a linear, logical manner. As if he had years of military training for half of his nineteen years of life, he established his own routine entering my office, shaking my hand and spending only a minute in pleasantries, always addressing me as Dr. Carpenter and inquiring how I was before he pulled out a folded piece of notebook paper with no more than five or six bullet points with the topics listed that he wished to address in his fifty minutes. Today the only exception to the routine was that he carried in a black athletic duffle bag with bold white cursive letters reading Midtown Athletic Club emblazoned on both sides.

"I apologize, but I didn't want to be late. I really need to find my allergy medication that I think is somewhere in this bag. That lakefront effect really hits me here in Cleveland." He sorted through the contents and pulled out a prescription bottle. "Ah, here it is. I thought I saw it when I worked out the other day. Okay, now we can get going." In one quick move, he screwed off the top, popped a pill into his mouth, followed by a quick gulp from his water bottle. He then placed the duffel bag at the side of his chair.

"How are you doing, Dr. Carpenter." Trenton, in contrast to his mother, wasted very little time getting settled. "You look nice today." I looked down at the ruffle dress as if reminding myself that I had on clothes. It was most likely the lemon yellow color that Trenton found attractive. His own safari jacket hung loosely over jeans evidencing his love of fashion and his own personal style.

"Thank you, Trenton." I said a bit too cheerily. Trenton, like his father Jamal, evoked gushing. Better to get right into the session. "What's on your mind today?" It was our third session in a week and a half, and I suspected we would be covering his high school experience since he had spent the first session on his childhood experience and the next on elementary school and all of the associated angst with growing up biracial. In both sessions neither of us uttered the word gay or broached the topic of sexual orientation.

"There's something I have to tell you." He pushed his torso forward, his knees brushing against the low coffee table positioned between us. He used the table to stabilize his knees that were shaking with nervous energy. "There's this doctor confidentiality thing, right?"

"Well, of course... what you tell me as a patient is kept in confidence," I assured him. "Unless, of course, you are thinking of harming yourself or harming someone else, then we would need to talk about the extent of that confidentiality."

"Nah, it's nothing like that ... at least not me harming anyone." His eyes were fixed on the circular table as I tried unsuccessfully to make eye contact. Redirecting my gaze away, I hoped to encourage his disclosure. He quickly looked up staring until I made eye contact again.

"You know I'm gay." That couldn't possibly be the information he wanted to protect under the confidentiality seal. My gaydar had improved over the years, but even back in the day, despite what Jessica and Tina might think, I might have been able to spot this brother as gay.

"That is obvious, and I've never tried to hide that." He chuckled. "I don't think I could if I wanted to. When I was in high school, I became really cool with being who I am. At the same time, my mom became obsessed with trying to tell me that my dad might not be my biological father."

"Obsessed? What was her obsession like?"

"Oh, she would just really bring it up all the time. Whenever I would want to talk about a friend at school who came out to me or someone I had a crush on, she would bring it up. I mean she doesn't always follow the line of thinking in a conversation really well anyway, you know how she can get lost on a topic," he smiled, fondly thinking about his mother's communication style, "but it was almost like a stimulus-response reaction. When I would talk about being gay she would start talking about my dad. Or rather casting doubts about my dad as my father."

"Did you ever make her aware of that pattern?" Maybe Rachel questioned Jamal's own sexual orientation. Was Tina right about Jamal being on the down-low? But that might confirm rather than deny his paternity. But there is no correlation between gay parents having gay children, but Rachel wouldn't think like that.

"You know Mom. She never gave me a direct answer and even denied that she even brought up the subject a lot. When I went off to college, she was tripping. Dad worked all the time. I mean all the time. Dad's got more money than God it seems, and she was shopping like she had seven days to redecorate the world. She was miserable and really didn't have any real friends. Her girlfriends were more like those Real Housewives women than real people. They weren't really what you would call sisters. Man, one even tried to hit on me a bunch of times. That was fricking weird. Mom would get real giddy when Uncle Don came around. Then she started talking more about Uncle Don and what a good friend he could be to her. Started hanging out with his assistant from work just so she could know his every move." A moment of silence came between his narrative and the next statement.

"I used to hang with Uncle Don, and I couldn't tell if she was just jealous. Uncle Don was real cool about my being gay, and we used to go clubbing together. He wanted to keep me safe...but you know, sometimes I think that was just an excuse for him to get out there. Uncle Don seemed liberated when he was at the club." He abruptly stopped, and the silence in the room hung like a chandelier.

"Did you start to believe that your Uncle Don might be your father?" With a lump in my throat, I recalled Jessica's pained look when she talked about their breakup. Surely, finding out Don had a son would not cause a breakup? Trenton's voice once again filled the room intruding on a connector thought that maybe they broke up because Don was gay.

"I'm sorry." The thought startled me back to the reality of the session. Trenton stopped midsentence. "I'm sorry. I was still back on what you were saying about your Uncle Don enjoying being with you at the club. Do you mind repeating what you said?"

"I knew what I said must not have registered with you." He swallowed and repeated. "When Mom was on one of her rampages insisting that Don was my father, I started looking for documents to confirm that he wasn't and stumbled on to information about what might have happened to Uncle Don. I think my father might have had something to do with his death."

CHAPTER 12

Parking at the Renaissance Hotel was always a challenge. Within thirty minutes of the cocktail hour for an event, the adjacent hotel lot was full. On Saturday evenings when the Cleveland Indians were playing—win or lose to their loyal fans—and there was a sold-out concert at the Convocation Center, you were destined to walk a few blocks in three-inch heels in addition to paying three times the regular parking rate at any lot near the hotel.

"Hey, the lot near Johnny's is open and that is actually even better than valet parking at the Renaissance," Jon told me. Despite our plans to get here right at the top of the hour, arriving within a half hour of the start time was congratulatory. We rushed from a day of errands and plans for Jon's extended trip and considered ourselves doing good just to be able to get here. Skipping the cocktail hour wouldn't work well for parking, and being preoccupied with Trenton's revelations, I didn't feel like making any small talk. I would have preferred the walk to the hotel even in heels. It was a good possibility that Rachel might be at the fundraiser since it would be impossible for Joy to prevent her from an opportunity to showcase to a crowd in formal wear and parade down an imaginary red carpet. If I saw her, it would be hard to share the same space without interrogating her.

"I'll drop you at the door and go park." Jon offered.

"You are such a gentleman." The thank you managed to extricate itself from my anticipatory anxiety of possibly seeing Rachel.

"Not really. Just took a look at those shoes on your feet and don't want to hear you grumbling and whining and carrying on about..."

"Okay, okay," I interrupted, laughing. "You could have just taken the credit and accepted it as a complement. No one would ever have known."

"I would have... and it wouldn't be, as you would say... emotionally honest."

"I'll be in the lobby waiting." Jon sped away eager to get one of the remaining spaces in the lot directly across the street. I stepped out of the car just in time to come face to face with the Nelsons... Rachel, Jamal, and Trenton.

"I thought you would be here. Joyce tries to get money out of everyone for this fundraiser. She used to even make us buy a couple of tables from Atlanta. She would use the tickets for the hospital staff to recognize their year-long efforts. Isn't that right, Jamal?" Jamal didn't even attempt to answer Rachel, his usual winner smile unnoticeable. Had Trenton used our session as a practice confessional and then conveyed his accusations to him?

"It's good to see you all dressed up and maybe we will get to see you on the dance floor. But then again maybe there won't be much dancing 'cause this is a Catholic hospital event. Oh, but that's Baptists who don't dance and that's more of a south thing. The folks in the north don't seem to interpret the Bible the way they do where we live. You here by yourself, Dr. Carpenter? Maybe you'll be at our table. Oh, how rude of me!" Rachel pronounced as she pulled Trenton closer to her.

"This is my son, Trenton." She double-winked and with her other hand pulled Jamal over.

"And you may remember my husband Jamal." She winked again. "We'll just leave the professional relationship we have behind tonight and start fresh. You can just be a close family friend from many years ago." She paused, delighted with her interpretation.

"That's actually the truth." My mouth dropped open in a natural attempt to get some air. I had not taken a breath since I laid eyes on the Nelsons. Rachel continued to talk, barely noticing my stupor.

"Don't be so scared, Sister, I mean Doctor. We won't tell any secrets tonight." Rachel winked again.

"Rachel, you're embarrassing Dr. Carpenter." In his CEO take-charge mode, Jamal moved Rachel to the escalator leading to the ballroom and motioned for Trenton to follow. "Dr. Carpenter, enjoy your evening." He nodded and lifted his chin in the direction of the door. Following his line of sight, I glimpsed Jon making his way through a sea of tuxedoed white men.

"You look shaken." Jon guided me to the escalator, avoiding the small mob that had convened in the entryway.

"We are not staying long, and if we end up at the same table with Joy's family then we can't stay."

"We have to leave?" Leaning in close, he matched my whisper.

"Trust me. We just can't be at the same table." With years of high-profile individuals as my patients, Jon knew better than to probe when I asked for his trust.

"What's our excuse if we need to leave?" Jon was quickly on program and didn't miss a beat to strategize. We entered the ballroom and were given instructions to move to table six. Viewing the two empty chairs at the table that was otherwise populated with hospital administrators, I saw Fr. Randy's welcome face sitting next to the hospital chaplain.

I breathed a sigh of relief audible to Jon. "We still don't need to stay long. I have an early flight tomorrow, remember?" He responded. His eyes that penetrated mine received my deep gratitude. Jon was leaving town tomorrow for a conference on the West Coast followed by an accreditation site visit. We had just discussed the late afternoon departure in the car on the way to the Charity Ball, so the early flight excuse would only be a half lie.

Randy leaned into the table to get my attention, rolling his eyes to let me know that he had had enough of Fr. O'Malley's conversation in the short time they were seated. I managed a knowing smile and turned my attention with the rest of the six hundred guests to Aaron Sullivan, a prominent real estate attorney and chair of the hospital's board of trustees. Joy made her way to the podium and presented the customary welcome but with a personal flair that rivaled Oprah Winfrey. The table where she returned was notable, not just because it held center stage in the large ballroom, but because Rachel's couture fuchsia strapless gown nestled between the custom-fitted midnight black tuxedos of her husband and son rendered an Academy Awards quality to the department store formals and rental tuxedos of the majority of the guests seated in the double-digit-numbered tables.

It had been hard to read Trenton's emotions in the lobby as he stood stoically with his parents whom he suspected had something to do with the death of Don Davenport. I found myself speechless being so close to what could be real evidence and not just conjecture. It would certainly clear Jessica's name while at the same time possibly put the sister of a long-time friend who was my patient in jail. Or maybe Jamal's upset over Don's death was not really grief but guilt? Suspecting that Don had undue influence over Trenton's sexual orientation, I thought he had just as much reason to be angry with Don as Rachel.

"Dr. Carpenter, I've just read your latest book and really enjoyed it, if you can say one enjoys reading self-help books.

Perhaps insightful is the word that better fits what I am trying to say." Concerns about a murderer or possibly two murderers being at this benefit dinner left little cognitive space for even kind words about my book. I managed a strained smiled to the vice-president of human resources for the hospital system seated next to me.

"I actually have a brother that I read the book for, so I could give him some advice. And," she chuckled, "Sr. Joy told me that she was seating you and Dr. Hoffman at this table so I brushed up a bit on your background. I'm not married, but my brother's marriage is challenging right now. You know, women's intuition... I don't think he would ever suspect his wife being unfaithful, but that is why after reading your book, I have to be able to tell him to wake up and smell the Starbucks."

"I'm glad it was helpful." The voice quality of my first words uttered since experiencing the lobby gathering of suspects for Don Davenport's murder sounded particularly robotic.

"Oh, it was. It was. I'm just waiting to stage a time to talk to my brother about it and share my insights." Over the loud chatter in the room, the ring tone for a text message on my phone was audible to those seated at the table.

"Oh, I'm sorry. That's mine. I forgot to turn it off." I apologized to the other guests and looked at Jon wondering if he was clever enough to stage my phone to ring as an excuse for us to leave. Tina's picture appeared on the screen as I pressed

Ignore. "It's Tina," I said to Jon. "She wants me to call her. Remind me to call her on the way home." A minute later the phone rang. As I attempted to silence the phone, Tina's picture appeared. "Excuse me," I said, rising from my seat to move toward the side exit door.

"Tina, I'm at an event. Can I call you back later? We're planning to slip out and leave early."

"Ah, no. You're my one phone call. I've been arrested."

"You're funny, Tina. I know I owe you a phone call and really will call you back. I'll make this an excuse to get out of here in an hour or so."

"No, I'm not kidding," She pleaded. "I couldn't call Melody and I didn't dare call Jessica 'cause her butt's on the line as well. These assholes are serious about holding me here until we can clear this up. You've got to come spring me and keep this quiet so my rep doesn't get creamed. I mean this might give me some street creds with my rapper clients, but not with the design world. Oh, my God, I can't believe this."

"Tina, this isn't funny, especially with all that's going on with Jess." It was odd that Tina would go to this extreme to keep me on the phone. I expected her next line to be "Psych"—instead, the words that came sounded like a lone wolf scream.

"Kathy, they really think I had something to do with killing Don."

CHAPTER 13

The glass partition that separated the public from the residents in the Atlanta Detention Facility provided a glimpse of the activity that occurred around the corner in the triage center.

"I can see Tina. Thank God, she's okay. At least she looks okay. I can't even imagine what last night must have been like for her," I said, as Randy and I walked over to the counter now that Cindy, who identified herself as the facility's manager, had left her desk. I was sure that we weren't the first individuals who came in with a little bit of attitude that a loved one was being held behind bars, and we certainly wouldn't be the last ones. Forget any notion of customer service or a philosophy that the customer was always right. We weren't exactly customers with complaints, and she treated us with disdain from the moment we walked in the door.

"She's a trooper and will be okay. Just don't pounce on her with questions as soon as you see her... at least in the first few minutes. Give her some time. She'll let you know the full story in time," Randy reassured me. We both returned to the worn burgundy cushioned armchairs and I began nervously rubbing the wood frame.

Like kids who had been sent to the principal's office, we knew better than to ask how much longer we could expect before we were released. I didn't dare ask about Tina, but some information on what was happening behind those doors would be helpful. Impulsively I approached the counter, crestfallen that Tina was no longer in view.

"Funny, you could have fooled me looking like you real smart, but somehow I don't think you are. You don't get it when I say you don't need to be approaching my space until I tell you." Cindy had appeared like a genie from a bottle giving me no time to scurry back to my seat.

"I'm sorry. I'm just a little eager to see my sister." My apologetic tone did nothing to soften the wicked witch of the reformatory.

"Well you can just sat your little eager butt down until I say you can come up here and even look in my face." I considered whether or not this could be some kind of harassment charge, but then again she would most likely turn it around and I would be charged with harassment. After all, I was in her space… as she continued to remind me. Clapping her hands directly in my face, Cindy's shrill voice erased any pondering.

"Hey, what part of go sat your ass down do you not understand?" She punctuated each word with a sharp, pulsing beat.

I almost responded that I would be happy to *sit* down, but I didn't think she would appreciate the grammar lesson.

"Just get on back out there with your man. This is not your house and it certainly ain't your party, and unless it's your birthday you ain't special here."

"He's…not my man. He's a priest." I sputtered out.

"Excuse me. Excuse me."

"That's Fr. Randy. He's my pastor and a good friend of mine…and like my family; he came to help Tina out of this mess." She peered around my left side to glance at Randy who sat stoic and poker-faced.

"Like I said, you ain't special and I ain't in no way impressed. Everybody's got some apostle with some boot-leg tent on the corner of Auburn that they cleaned up and dragged in here to try and get special treatment." I turned to Randy, confused that she would mistake him with some kind of southern Christian revivalist preacher character from that Robert Duvall movie. Other than being black, Randy certainly looked like any other Catholic priest.

"Why do you have to be so mean?" I thought out loud. Wondering about her assessment of Randy not being a real priest made me curious about what motivated her to doubt my veracity. Heart palpitations signaled that my anger was seeping up. Thank God I had enough sense not to release my anger on her. It was better that I just stood there sounding like a Taylor Swift song.

Ironically, questioning her meanness caused her to laugh. But it was the kind of laugh you might hear in a dark graveyard before the vampire sucked blood out of you.

"Fuck you," I said, surprising myself and apparently Cindy as well. Anger oozed out of my pores.

"Excuse me." She responded uncharacteristically.

"Stop messing with my sister, Cindy." Tina came out of the door unaccompanied. Other than the wrinkled hem of her shirt, flat hair, and absent the fake eyelashes that permanently made their home on her eyelids, one would never know that Tina had just spent a night in jail. She poked Cindy on her shoulder and surprisingly, she didn't turn and scratch Tina's eyeballs out.

"Uh…and you better behave 'cause brother man over there really is a priest. I heard what you said about the tent minister on Auburn. I know that guy," Tina high-fived Cindy.

"You so crazy!" Tina proclaimed as they both guffawed. "Girl, let me bust out of here." She gave Cindy a brief but affectionate hug.

"Being here might give me some street creds with my rapper clients, but I could have just *said* I was here and really wasn't." Cindy smirked and pressed a button that sounded a buzzer releasing Tina to join us in the now-filled waiting room.

Randy took the few steps from his seat to meet Tina in the center of the room. The whiff of Tina's Eternity perfume interrupted the locked stare exchanged with Cindy. She broke and gave me a sheepish smile, piling more confusion on my brain.

"How are you?" Randy comfortingly said to Tina, pulling her away a couple of feet to examine her closely. "You came out just in time. I thought we might end up having to leave Kathy here."

Tina laughed, pulled me into the embrace with Randy and whispered, "Actually I got hooked up and still have some basuco from last night so I am feeling pretty good right about now." Randy laughed at what I assumed was a joke. I've been pretty good defining words from context since my second grade vocabulary lessons with Sr. Emily and quickly assumed basuco was some kind of drug.

"Come on, let's get out of here. I don't even watch *Prison Break* and have no desire to start my television career being on that show." Nestled between Randy and me, Tina locked arms and directed us to the door with a quick turn to Cindy who waved in response to her barely audible, "Ciao!"

I was glad that Randy had come with me. The make and model of the rental car we drove here eluded me. Between my freaking out on even the thought of Tina sleeping overnight in a jail instead of her designer bedroom and Randy's futile attempts to manage my anxiety along with his concern, we were lucky that we got here safely. Randy lifted the car key, pressing the entry key until a midnight-blue Chevy Malibu blinked.

"How do you know Cindy?" I couldn't resist that question.

"You know I'm really mad at that Cindy. In less than five minutes she got you to say fuck after all my years of training. It's like divorcing some crazy man and then he takes all that good home training and straightens up and uses it with the next woman he marries."

Grateful that Tina was still very much herself, I opened the door of the back seat, and began to enter it when Tina moved me aside. "No, you get in the front. I'm exhausted and need to just spread out here in the back of this Chevy that will be considerably more comfortable than that cot last night." She jumped in still chatting. "And, no, I don't know Cindy, just met her last night when she came in and processed my release papers."

"Well, I'm really glad to hear she was friendly to you. She was crabby with us when we came in."

"She was crabby with me too until she found out I knew Tony, then she became my best friend."

"Who's Tony?" Randy turned to me and smiled, acknowledging that I had begun my interview process and turned his attention back to the road.

"Some dinosaur who keeps stalking me after the one and only date we will ever have. I told Jessica that those old-timers, match-maker websites attract nothing but sex-starved geezers." Tina propped her legs on the passenger window avoiding the handles and window switches.

"Oh, gee… did he try to rape you?" Maybe Cindy had a

similar experience with him that caused her to quickly bond with Tina.

Tina lifted her head up and through the strands of Spanish wavy hair weave came laughter. “Oh, God no! He was one of those fifty-year-old, born-again virgins—after being married twice,” she quickly added. “The date lasted exactly sixty-seven minutes and he sends me a picture of himself in his usher uniform going to church the next day and then he has been texting me to go out again every month since that date. He’s like a bad penny that keeps showing up in your wallet. But good thing I just ignored him instead of formally dumping him ’cause we’re actually going to continue to need his help.”

“We are?”

“Yep. He’s got strong connections,” Tina laid back and closed her eyes, “and he knows his business.”

“What’s his business?” Randy and I echoed.

“He’s a crime scene cleaner-upper,” Tina murmured and rolled on her side and fell instantly asleep.

CHAPTER 14A

"I don't think you should be here and associating with me since there's probably a couple of cops outside in a surveillance van."

Tina hugged Jessica as I ran to the window to check for an unmarked police car. Jessica arrived at Tina's loft minutes after we called with the news that Tina had been released. The two continued to embrace, whispering words of comfort around a shared nightmare in which they both were now equally entwined.

"It's a joke, Kath," Randy said, dropping my oversize leather tote near the sofa table in Tina's living room, the contents of which were a blur after I rushed home from Joy's charity event to pack, luckily securing an early flight to Atlanta. Once again Randy demonstrated his lean-on-me friendship by clearing his calendar and accompanying me to Atlanta, which allowed Jon to leave for the conference in San Diego, knowing Tina and I were in good hands. Randy, equally concerned about Tina, couldn't have been held back from making the trip. He was uncharacteristically ready in a heartbeat. Blessed assurance, our worst nightmare remained in our imagination as Tina's ebullience got her through the night and an on-line dating match turned out to be her salvation. Glancing at the phone, it reminded me that I needed to call Mom and let her know that Tina was okay.

"Geez! Mom has been blowing up my phone, calling every two minutes. Kath, do me a favor and let her know I am okay, I am going to take a quick shower."

"You read my mind. I'll do it right after a quick check-in with the office." With gratitude I watched Tina with Jess in tow as they left the room. It was really a selfish act for me to be here, since my anxiety would be out the roof if I were sitting in my office attempting to treat and lend emotional support to any patient.

"I'm sprung and free!" Tina returned from her bedroom in under twenty minutes folded in a thick white terry cloth robe and filling the room with a lavender fragrance. Jessica finally let Tina out of her sight and returned to the kitchen to whip up western omelets. Randy managed microwave bacon as I completed a three-way call with Mom and Dana, filling them in on Tina's condition and status with the law.

"No, Mom, as far as we know, there was no basis for whatever probable cause they thought they had. So, she's cleared." I lip synced Tina to question if she wanted to talk to Mom. She shook her head defiantly and mouthed "please, no" back as I covered the mouthpiece so Mom would not hear me chuckling.

"Mom, she's fine. Just a little exhausted. She'll give you a call when she's rested. Um…yes, we still have to pray for Jess," I whispered, not wanting Jess to hear that although Tina might not be a viable suspect, Jess remained a suspect unless someone stepped up to take credit for Don's alleged murder. I hoped with time Trenton might be more specific about his family's involvement. Dana picked up on the cue and got Mom to wrap up the call assuring her that all of us could talk more later in the day.

The meal's welcomed entry into our empty stomachs also provided a good excuse for silence. If Tina were a patient of mine, I would probably ask if she was experiencing a deeper emotional connection with her best friend right now, or if she held anger toward her for not heeding her advice and leaving Don sooner than she had. After all, it was the fact that Tina had lent money to Jess and the checks were deposited in both Jess's and Don's account that caused her to be suspect, called into the station to be questioned, and then held overnight until her attorney called. Maybe Tina was kicking herself for getting involved, but Jess was family, and it would be hard for any of us to turn our back on her, especially during a crisis like this one. Any one of us would have loaned her money and gladly suffered the same consequences. There certainly was no evidence of regret or anger in Tina's demeanor. I glanced at my sister and gave a grateful smile.

"I am so glad that you are okay and the case was dismissed." I thought aloud catching Tina's eyes only briefly as she glanced down. Jess gave me an empty stare and then quickly turned to Tina obviously struggling with both relief for Tina and the deeper realization that she now stood alone in the lineup of suspects.

"We're all glad that this is moving forward," Randy said. "And speaking of moving forward, I am going to head over to the Diocesan Offices to see Dave before I catch an early flight back."

"I thought you planned to stay for at least a couple of days. You must have cleared your calendar so why rush back now." I was looking forward to some down time, and Randy's easy humor was a calming presence for Jess, Tina, and especially me. "Besides, Dave is probably not in town and knowing him, if he's around he's probably double-booked with meetings." Fr. Dave Root served as judicial vicar for court of appeals for the Atlanta diocese, and as another one of the 250 black priests in the US, he and Randy were very close friends.

"No need to worry. If he isn't around, I have other business I need to take care of," Randy noticed that I was taken aback and hurriedly continued. "We communicated by text earlier. I let him know I was in town and he fortunately has some time now, so I am heading out and leaving you lovely women to watch some *Oprah* and some daytime television."

"Oprah's show has been off the air." Tina laughed and gave Randy a hug. Jess followed and repeated the gesture. You would have thought we picked Tina up from a cruise vacation instead of jail the way they both took in Randy being here and leaving so quickly.

"No reruns? Well, turn on *Lifetime* or whatever women like to watch, get some rest, go to a spa, read *O Magazine*. That's still around, isn't it? Anyway, y'all are adults. Do what you want, and Kath, take the time to relax and spend some time with your sisters. I will see you later this week."

They had cooked bacon for breakfast but I could smell fish in the room. As soon as Randy pulled away, I suspected we wouldn't be watching any daytime television. I intended to have some straight talk with my sisters and find out what was really behind Tina's arrest.

CHAPTER 14B

"I don't think you should be here and associating with me since there's probably a couple of cops outside in a surveillance van." That should send Kathy flying to the window to check if there was a van outside. I could have planned this better and staged Brian and Glen out there in a black sedan. Kath would have flown out there like a tornado ready to swoop them up and fling them across Atlanta. Attempting to give Jess an update with Kathy's watchful eye and attentive ears was proving to be almost impossible.

"It's a joke, Kath," Randy said, dropping Kathy's oversize leather tote near the sofa table in the living room. Randy did a good job of getting Kathy here without her calling in favors to get me out of jail from everyone from the Pope in exchange for all those years spent in the convent, to Obama for all the millions she must have pumped into his campaign. But Randy was blowing my time with Jess by not keeping Kathy distracted. Tightening my grip on Jess, I turned her ear to my lips, "she's buying the arrest and we have to get a hold of Tony pronto." Jess looked relieved when I released my grip, but I know I tripped her out bringing up Tony.

"Tony?" Jessica's announcer voice didn't know how to come in low key, so I impulsively pinched her hard. The pinch not only shut her up, but made her grimace in a way that Kathy looked sympathetically at us, probably psychoanalyzing that we were in some kind of shared emotional pain.

"Come with me while I change," I whispered to Jess as Kath moved toward the tote that Randy had just put down, giving me enough time to motion to Jess and confirm that she heard me. The vibration of the phone in my jeans pocket released an automatic reflex and scared the bejeebees out of me.

"Geez! Mom has been blowing up my phone calling every two minutes. Kath, do me a favor and let her know I am okay, I am going to take a quick shower."

"You read my mind. I'll do it right after a quick check-in with the office."

Perfect. Giving Kathy a task to accomplish interrupted the surveillance she managed to keep until Jess and I disappeared into the bedroom.

Jess headed straight for the bed, sat down, and began to speak. I immediately shushed her, knowing Kathy's x-ray hearing, and quickly turned on the shower to camouflage our voices.

"Tina, I told you this wasn't a good idea and we just needed to be straight with Kathy. She's not dumb you know."

"No, girl, you don't know Sister Nun like I do. There was no way she would break confidentiality about a patient. We had to up the ante. And it's working!" Jess's dubious look told me she did not agree.

"We should have just asked her. She'll be pissed when she finds out you intentionally framed yourself when they questioned you, and it could get me in more trouble. They know I was at the scene of the crime, I mean accident, and you didn't have to tell them you had borrowed my car. There was no possible way that witness could mistake me for you."

"She doesn't need to know," Jess shook her head from side to side, still not buying my perfect scheme. "Trust me, once she realizes she might have information that could get me permanently off the hook, actually both of us off the hook, since she believes I'm implicated as well, even if it is something about one of her dear patients, she'll work with us."

"How do you know that this leads to one of her patients?"

"Just a hunch." Jess groaned, moaned, and shook her head.

"No, the tight brother from Atlanta that I met at Fr. Randy's anniversary party was really hung up about Don's death. I high-tailed it out of there to get back here to you, so I didn't get the full story. When I talked with Kathy later, she consoled me, saying that Randy said that guy was confident, and she quoted him as saying 'confident' that you would be acquitted. I know Kathy is seeing someone from Atlanta because she casually asked me about where Virginia

Highlands was, and when I asked her why, she told me that her nun friend Joy has a sister who lived there. Then it clicked. The white woman that Don was cheating on you with…" Jessica cringed, "…that was with Don that night was probably Joy's sister. Remember I said she looked familiar? She was probably the same white woman you saw that night. And the same woman at the funeral that I thought might even be Sr. Joy. It all fits."

"*That* is what you were going on when you decided to get arrested? The fact that a friend of Fr. Randy's who knew Don, was from Atlanta? And Kathy might have a patient that might be the white woman you are still convinced was after Don? Oh, my God, Tina! How lame is that? And there were a number of white women around Don's complex that night. He lived in a white neighborhood!"

"I know what I saw Jess. That white woman just wasn't an old 'friend' as Don claimed. Anyway, no point in repeating that conversation even though that part is true; I know what I saw. And it was probably her at the funeral. And you did tell me you saw a white woman quickly leave the building that night. I admit though, the other part does sounds a bit lame, especially when I say it out loud…" My sure footing was slipping a bit. "…but I know my sister, and I have a hunch here that she is sitting on information that could help us and doesn't even realize it."

Jess was going to shake the brains right out of her head disagreeing with me.

"Stop shaking your head like that. If I am wrong, then we really haven't lost anything and we would go on record for trying. Just follow my lead on this one. I promised you I would get you through this. Trust me. Okay?" That stopped the head shaking. She rose and gave me a hug, and there might have been a hint of hope in her eyes. "Now scoot before she comes snooping in here. I've got to run through this shower."

"I'm sprung and free!" I announced loudly so that Kath would get freaked out again that I had spent the night in jail. Well, technically I was there, so I wasn't completely playing with her emotions. Smelling the bacon Randy was pulling out of the microwave made me instantly ravenous.

"No, Mom, as far as we know there was no basis for whatever probable cause they thought they had. So, she's cleared." Kathy began to hand me the phone to talk to our mother, the woman that was the well from which all of Kathy's anxiety sprung.

"Please, no!" I mouthed to her, making sure Fr. Randy didn't see me. He was pretty cool, but disrespecting your mother in front of a priest had to deduct some points for getting into heaven, and I needed all the easy points I could get.

"Mom, she's fine. Just a little exhausted. She'll give you a call when she's rested. Um…yes, we still have to pray for Jess," Kathy turned away, obviously not wanting to upset Jess.

That was a good thing 'cause we were going to need all of her sympathies.

Randy was busy texting and eating. Jess was staying distracted so she wouldn't say anything to make me leap across the kitchen island counter and duct tape her mouth, and I couldn't think of a thing to say that Sister Nun would not turn over and analyze a hundred times, so I ate. The silence was long and uncomfortable.

"I am so glad that you are okay and the case was dismissed." Kathy finally broke the silence I wasn't about to make eye contact with her and tried to distract Jess from doing the same.

"We're all glad that this is moving forward ... and speaking of moving forward, I am going to head over to the Diocesan Offices to see Dave before I catch an early flight back." Good ole' Randy to the rescue. Thank you.

"I thought you planned to stay for at least a couple of days. You must have cleared your calendar so why rush back now." Kathy began her adult pout. "Besides, Dave is probably not in town and knowing him, if he's around he's probably double-booked with meetings."

"No need to worry. If he isn't around, I've got other business I need to take care of." Kathy looked confused and was instantly thinking it was insensitive for Randy to plan a meeting when my butt would have been stuck in jail. It would have been insensitive if I hadn't called him last night and confessed to him that I voluntarily offered some information that might have led them to believe that I might know something more about Don's death. At first I thought he was just being sympathetic to me attempting to go to any extreme to help Jess, but he must have his own investigation going on. I was talking about that cheating white woman who might have been there when Don died and trying to be careful not to spill the beans that Jessica's butt was sitting in the car and probably saw her when he got all distracted. Randy was suddenly eager to come to Atlanta, seemingly to support Kathy. But if you ask me, he was on his own mission.

"We've been communicating by text. I let him know I was in town and fortunately he has some time now, so I am heading out and leaving you lovely women to watch some Oprah and some daytime television."

"Oprah's show has been off the air." Brother man was funny or maybe he did live under a rock and not in the priest house. Jess and I gave him a hug, eager to get our investigation started.

"No reruns? Well, turn on *Lifetime* or whatever women like to watch, get some rest, go to a spa, read *O Magazine*. That's still around isn't it? Anyway, y'all are adults. Do what you want, and Kath, take the time to relax and spend some time with your sisters. I will see you later this week."

Kathy turned and gave me and Jess her Sister Nun look. Jess was right. She was not as naive as I hoped she might be.

CHAPTER 15

Tony Labella's bottom lip was only inches from his plate as he used the fork to shovel Tina's gumbo into his mouth at about ten scoops per second. In my mind, a crime scene cleaner conjured up a science guy nerdy type, someone who had a degree in forensic science and used the crime scenes as his personal laboratory for scholarly pursuits. Tony did not fit that image at all. He was proud of the fact that with only an online course in blood-borne pathogen training and a few years as a janitor at the Bank of America Plaza, he was now making six figures and was the highest paid crime cleaner in the city. He boasted of a personal relationship with the Atlanta City Chief of Police and that he was often called to the scene before the lieutenant.

Absent any kind of scientist white lab coat and garbed in a brown bib shirt with buttons, Levi jeans and boots, he appeared as if he was headed for a day on the ranch rather than for cleaning up crime scenes. After he received the call inviting him to lunch, I imagined Tony scurrying around his bedroom anxiously putting together one of his best outfits to impress Tina. The outfit was only one of the indicators for why a date with Tina would last just over an hour. Their gregarious spirit might have penetrated across the internet chat room, and an online dating service software program might have deemed them a good match, but placed together in the same room, as a physical couple, they were quite odd.

"You know I still can't believe you called me," the rhythm of Tony's eating was not to be interrupted by his need for conversation. Thus, Tina and I were subjected to witnessing the mastication of shrimp, sausage, and chicken as he spoke. It was not a pretty sight, so I automatically lowered my head every time he began to speak.

"I thought I was dreaming." He gazed up at Tina who still stood by the stove after turning off the burner from under the leftover gumbo she had warmed. "You are in my dreams, you know."

"I'm glad your dreams have been pleasant." Tina flirted unabashedly and got quickly to the point of why she was enduring this visit. "But you know my sister and I have not had a good night's sleep since our good friend died." I quickly looked up and then quickly looked down to hide any puzzled glance at Tina's feigned grieving. I had agreed to meet Tony and hear what information he might have about the evidence involved with Don's death, but my improvisations were not as polished as Tina's were, and I sensed that I was about to be dragged into a story she was concocting and that my expression would be a dead giveaway for a lie.

"You had a friend that died?" Tony actually paused for a second to lean back on the chair, and then quickly reached for his glass of sweetened ice tea. "Gee, I'm sorry about that." His voice carried genuine compassion. He might be someone obsessed with blood and guts, but he also had a heart.

"Oh, it was so tragic." Tina heavily sighed, and I actually thought I saw her eyes tearing up. "We've known him forever... since he was from Cleveland. And Kathy has been particularly close to him over the years." I gulped, hopefully not too loudly. Tina quickly continued to distract Tony who was looking empathetically at me. "That's why she came to Atlanta. We needed to be together since we are both trying to make meaning out of his terrible death."

It was better for me to sit and say nothing, since I had no idea what direction Tina was taking this conversation. After some prodding, Jess had finally admitted that Tina's arrest was more "informal" as she called it. Tina stuck to her story about how fearful and distraught she was from being questioned by the police and even remotely connected to a murder. I did not doubt the veracity of her fear. The phone call she made to me was genuine, but I suspected that it was because her own investigation of Don's death got her in a bit too deep and she panicked. How she actually ended up staying overnight in jail was still a mystery. I decided to stop pushing her for the full story... for now. As with most Tina escapades, the truth, like cream, had a tendency to rise to the top. What her arrest and her quickly established friendship with the facility manager, Cynthia, did manage to accomplish was confirmation that Tony Labella was indeed involved in the Davenport case clean up. Tina was definitely using that data to her advantage today.

"You know they really thought the guy offed himself for at least a few days." Tina moved closer to Tony which did the trick, encouraging him to talk even more.

"Oh, really? It might actually be more comforting for it to be that he was so depressed or in some kind of trouble that he actually took his life rather than someone intentionally murdering him." Tina scooped more gumbo into Tony's bowl. I scowled at her, wondering if she honestly believed that.

"I mean, at least he had some kind of control and wanted to die versus someone cutting him off." Tina shrugged her shoulders as if to confirm that suicide was a better option in this case.

"Oh, somebody wanted him gone all right." Tony began shoveling the gumbo in again without the benefit of an occasional napkin pat. "There were a number of prints on his clothing that said someone was really close to him when he plunged. Close enough that if they wanted to pull him back they could. You know most of the clean-ups that I do are suicides. Even though I've been in the business for years, you only get one, maybe two, high-profile murder cases like this one. This is my third," he boasted. "So, I guess I'm lucky if you want to call it luck. Suicide clean-ups are pretty routine... disinfecting, odor removal, air infiltration, mattress removal, carpet replacement." Tony went down his checklist. "You get a murder and you know the difference. And this one was not a suicide. My guy Andy was on the case so I got to help analyze the room. Most cops really treat us crime cleaners like janitors, but Andy really respects my opinion since I know a bit more than most people do about forensic matters... and not just the stuff from *CSI* and *Law & Order*. I read a lot. Like the real forensic science stuff... textbooks and all. Even took a forensic science course at Herzing Community College. Got an A. Best grade in the class. Professor really liked having an older guy like me to share all my experiences and knowledge with the kids who were just there fantasizing about being like that character Catherine Willows on *CSI*."

"So Sherlock, what did you discover about our guy Don?" Tina cut him off, her patience waning and the lack of it evident through her sarcasm and casual attitude. Tony was absorbed both in his personal career assessment and the gumbo, so he didn't notice. Luckily, he got back on track, spilling all he knew about Don's death.

"There was evidence on the body of a struggle. It wasn't just a swimming pool plunge to the ground like a suicide would have been. That expensive Thomas Pink shirt was damaged in ways that don't happen in a splatter." Tina and I both cringed.

"What? A guy can't know a designer shirt without being

gay? I happen to have some style despite the fact that some might think I'm just a crime janitor." Tony brushed his hand over the brown bib button shirt that I had only seen as costumes in musicals like "Oklahoma" as evidence of designer taste. His personal fashion assessment confirmed that Tony was indeed the perfect candidate for the style show, *What Not to Wear.*

"I think you look mar-ve-lous!" Tina imitated the pronunciation of "marvelous" from an old Billy Crystal *Saturday Night Live* skit. She couldn't be serious—or was she? "So, tell me more, darling, about the evidence and who they might suspect pushed our dear friend." Not a trace of her momentary frustration and dislike for Tony's self-aggrandizement showed this time as Tina pumped Tony for more information. He easily fell into the trap.

"Hey, I can only speak about my clean-up process and not about any evidence." He straightened himself in the chair in his most professional stance. "Uhm... we aren't having this conversation, wink, wink." He tried to coordinate his fluttering eyelashes as he said wink, but was so out of sync he resembled someone on heavy psychotic medication experiencing tics. He didn't understand that the guise was by actually winking rather than saying the word "wink."

Tina grabbed the upholstered dining room chair next to his and moved closer in rapt attention. Tony smiled as if it were the beginning of foreplay. "Well," he slowly began, "there's a maintenance guy who they are watching closely 'cause he has a knack for being where he shouldn't be and might know more than he's fessing up. But the real juice is that they know that Mr. Davenport was hanging out with a young brother who, from his appearance, might be gay as well. Real good-looking young guy, light-skin-dude, probably mixed, dressed like the white boys in those fancy private schools. Real groomed." This time he noticed the puzzled look on both our faces, but he was only concerned about Tina's response.

"Not that there's anything wrong with being gay. Hey, I'm not homophobic. I'm Christian and all, and I'm not on the down-low or anything. A black man living in Atlanta can't help but have some kind of knowledge base about that lifestyle, if you know what I mean." Tina was obviously frustrated that we were once again side-tracked from getting real information, but if Tony believed that Don was gay, then perhaps the police were also under the impression that Don was possibly on the down-low.

"So they suspect a young brother who appears to be gay?"

"I don't know nothing about the suspects. Just know that there was at least one guy that we, I mean they, know of that was at his condo at least a few hours before his plunge. They got a positive identification from the ground's security cameras that the guy was someone Don was acquainted with because he had been there before." This was in some ways puzzling, but the pieces were coming together. This time Tony noticed my puzzlement.

"Hey, that's all I know... and even if I did know more I

couldn't say because, you know, I don't want to jeopardize the confidence placed in me by the few cops that seek my advice on these cases. You know, I am held to the same oath of silence as they are when they consult with me."

"We understand and appreciate that you shared with us what you did. I'm a psychologist and appreciate confidentiality." Treating Tony like the professional who knew the secret handshake was important if we needed to gather any necessary information in the future. In the moment that it took for me to use the word *psychologist,* I was thrust back into that identity as an image of Trenton flashed in my mind...young brother, obviously gay, in Don's apartment hours before his plunge. Almost about to blurt out that I knew it had to be Trenton, I gathered composure and said, "Tina, I believe we have had enough talk about this tragedy for today. Let's let Tony finish his lunch." Tina's dark brown eyes squinted at me as I continued.

"Tony, tell me, what do crime professionals do in the spare time when they are not working?" Tactfully, I changed the content of the conversation while keeping Tony talking. With years of bonding as sisters, Tina's eyes locking with mine confirmed that we had all that we needed to move forward.

CHAPTER 16

"You two are wonderful, and I could not have asked for better sisters had we been birthed from the same mother, but I really need you to leave my case alone and not get yourselves in trouble." The weight of the case had obviously taken a toll on Jessica's appearance, but most apparent was that the tone of her voice was absent the lilt and musical quality that had endeared friends and viewers to her.

"I have great attorneys who feel confident that this will all pass shortly, and you know it's funny and it sounds so cliché, but my faith is really sustaining me right now. It's like that song Kirk Franklin sings with the line 'you are my lawyer.'" Jessica began to hum a few lines of the gospel singer's "You Are," the lyrics listing all the ways Jesus is present in times of need.

"Well, Jesus spoke to me as well, and he told me to tell you that he loves you and all that good stuff, and that you will be all right, but he also said you got to get your ass up and fight back. We fall down, but we get up and kick some butt."

Tina began laughing at her liberal interpretation of Donnie McClurkin's gospel song, "We Fall Down."

"We fall down, but we get up! We fall down, but we kick butt!" She sang through her laughter. I joined in her laughter, glad to see that it brought a smile to Jessica's sullen face.

"We aren't going to tell you what we are doing. We just need to confirm a few things about Don's extracurricular activities." I tried to soften the reference to Don's gambling habit as it had been an especially sore point with Jessica. The media had shied away from buying into any confirmation of Jessica's culpability for Don's death, but they were merciless in their allegations about her having a gambling habit. There was plenty of guilt by association but they had combed her finances and made them public as proof that she and Don most likely suffered from a shared gambling addiction and that she was financially connected to the same sources as Don.

"I've told you both all that I know, and please, let's leave the investigation to those who do this for a living. Really, I appreciate it, but honestly, I am afraid you'll make matters worse." Jess's furrowed brow quickly vanished when she took in our disappointed expressions.

"How could we make it worse? You're the only one that they even have anything on, and despite the fact that what they have on you is worth a bunch of doo doo balls, these crazies will make something of it, and you will find yourself in one of those stories on *Dateline* with Lester Holt interviewing you, wearing an orange jumpsuit and trying to convince the world of your innocence." Tina's words were harsh, but I already saw the episode in my mind.

Jess began to cry. "Oh, Jessie," I quickly moved over next to her, shooting Tina a parenting look. "What Tina is trying to tell you is that anyone who is investigating this case doesn't necessarily have your best interest in heart. In fact, even your attorneys will work on your behalf but not because they love you…"

"They just love your money and the fact that they get to have their face on TV and be the next Johnnie Cochran." I signaled to Tina to let me handle this by shooting her another parent look.

"Yes, we love you and will work the best on your defense," Tina quickly stated, and for some reason this statement made Jessica laugh.

"I don't think I could stop you even if I had the strength to do so." Jessica twisted the striped dishtowel she had kept in her hands when we arrived. I was happy to see that there were a few dirty dishes in the sink, which must have meant that she had something to eat.

"This might be hard to talk about, but do you know if Don had a good friend, or even a friend for that matter, who someone would know was obviously gay?" Hearing the words come out of my mouth, it seemed like a strange question even to me.

"Uh…this is Atlanta, certainly he knew many gay men. I couldn't say that he was particularly close to anyone." Jessica paused. “Oh, God, you aren’t telling me that Don was on the down-low or anything like that?”

“No, no, no.” Tina quickly jumped in. “Patrick would have called him out a long time ago.” Patrick Simpson was Tina’s close friend and openly gay. Because he lived in Cleveland as a prominent educator and travelled to Atlanta often for social events, Tina was right in that he would have confided in her any knowledge if Don was attempting a closeted lifestyle. Tina would have been especially protective of Jessica and the world would have known.

“It’s nothing like that ... just exploring all options for who might have been involved in his life at the time of the accident. Apparently he was hanging with a young brother. Do you know anything about that?” I was again careful with trigger words like murder so as not to open the flood gates again. Surely Don must have made some references to Trenton if he was as close to the family as the Nelsons claimed.

“I really don’t know. And even if I did, I wouldn’t be able to recognize any of the people Don associated with around his,” she paused, swallowed, and sought the appropriate word, “his addiction. All of those men were around our age, or at least it looked that way from all of the pictures the police showed me during the questions. There were one or two young guys that were thrown in there, maybe even fake model pictures. I think they use those just to test how truthful you are because they may have been familiar faces from a magazine ad or something. I didn’t recognize any of them as even remotely associated with Don." She looked absent-mindedly out of the window behind where Tina and I stood peering at her. It must have seemed like another interrogation, only this one was friendly fire. Tina and I continued to stare at her. I began to wonder if it was best to keep probing. The momentary silence allowed her to recall a small but very significant fact.

"I knew he was mentoring a son of an old friend from Cleveland who he worked for... probably the only reason he was able to keep the job. He even loaned him money that he asked me to pay back. I think his name was Jamie, but I never ever met him, which is why, I admit, I really wasn't sure if he actually existed. He told me he was like an uncle to his kid especially because his father traveled a lot and his mother was a little wacky. Or at least that was one of his lame excuses he used when he was gone some evenings. I was finally supposed to actually meet the whole family. He never wanted me to meet them and then suddenly, change of heart; they were the answer to everything that was wrong. He insisted that he could clear everything up. Then I saw this document that was an affidavit of paternity on his desk and couldn't even deal with the possibility of that. That was it. I decided I couldn't take the lies anymore. Sounds stupid though," Jessica chastised herself. "And it will sound even more stupid in court if it gets to that point." The energy of her depression filled the air, waiting to descend like a rainstorm.

"It won't get to that." Tina said with confidence.

"It won't get to that." I echoed with even more confidence.

CHAPTER 17

"This is beginning to sound like the crazy stuff that you see on *Maury Povich* with the DNA test to discover who the baby daddy is." Tina responded to my attempt to encrypt the details of my story about Rachel's conviction that Don was Trenton's biological father. Even though Tina would eventually put two and two together and figure out that someone in the Nelson family, if not the entire family, was my patient, I nevertheless attempted to keep anonymity if not confidentiality. Tina, of course, would not just blindly do what I was asking; however, her resistance was stronger than anticipated. She was listening with such deep intensity that I became even more convinced that Trenton had indeed discovered the truth about his biological father, and it was the key to Don's possible murderer. There was motive enough. If Don was Trenton's biological father, it would have certainly set the course of the Nelson family down a very different personal and financial path.

"You are just going to have to trust that what I need you

to do will help Jess." I wasn't at all convinced that this path we were heading on was the right path, but with limited time and only a hunch, it was certainly worth checking out while I was still here in Atlanta.

"I know we are muddling through here, but I have a good hunch that all the dots will start connecting if I can just confirm this one fact."

"And that one little fact would be...?" Tina, rightly so, was refusing to go sailing into Midtown Athletic Club and just somehow accidently on purpose end up in the men's locker room.

"I can't disclose, okay fully disclose, where I got the information from, but I know that this individual happens to be a member of this gym, and I am certain, well reasonably certain, that an article of Don's might be in his locker." Tina's brow furrowed and her eyes, typically widely open, were compressed almost shut.

"So, let me see if I have this right. I'm supposed to go into the gym, somehow get past the desk and turnstile or whatever they have to keep people like me who are not members and do not have any badge or identification from getting in, and then go into the men's locker room, mind you—men's not women's locker room, find this guy's locker which you think might happen to be 911 because you vaguely recall him saying how the number seems to follow him in life, and get what might be an article from Don out of there." She didn't have to emphasize the "might." I knew this was a bit whacked, but didn't she just get herself arrested to gain information?

"Yes." I said, firmly hoping my confidence would put her a bit more at ease. "And there might be some medical records there as well if we are lucky." I flashed a fake smile.

"If *we* are lucky? Remember I just got out of jail." I looked at her sideways. "Well, I really was questioned, and then it took some time for them to clear me, so I was actually in jail. My ass is grass if I get caught again."

"All the better then, that I keep you a bit in the dark. That way I will be the one who is implicated this time. You will just have to say that I made you do it." Tina was right about the risk. I knew it was a long shot, but intuition was a strong internal function that had led me to some fruitful outcomes in the past. It had also led me down some paths that were complete disasters, but I didn't need to channel that energy right now.

Mr. T's voice bellowed from Tina's GPS instructing us that we were approaching Midtown Athletic Club on our right. I found the actor's voice jarring and distracting while trying to locate an unknown destination, but Tina found the programmed voice especially amusing when instead of announcing "recalculating" when one missed a turn, the voice announced "I pity the fool." It cracked her up laughing each time. Sometimes she made a wrong turn just to hear him say it.

Approaching the building, I recognized on one of its walls the silhouette of a running man as the logo from the duffle bag that Trenton brought into a session with him. When he searched for the allergy medicine he needed, the interesting logo became an easily identified brand when I Google-searched athletic clubs in Atlanta. Tina navigated the SUV into the large parking lot that was only a third occupied in the middle of the day. On second thought, it might have been better to try to retrieve a t-shirt that Trenton used as a confirmation source in his paternity test in the early morning or after work when the athletic club was crowded. Or maybe midday was the best time for an attractive, tall black woman with a Diana Ross-like weave, who would be my sister, *not* to be so noticeable in the men's locker room.

"Hey, how is this t-shirt tied to some paternity test? Am I picking up something bloody? I'm not putting anything bloody in my Gucci bag. Hand me your purse?" Tina had one leg out the door as she reached over the driver's seat for my brown leather purse that I got at half price with a pair of pumps at a DSW shoe store.

"It shouldn't be bloody." I chuckled at Tina's quick thinking about her aversion to anything that would interfere with her flawless designer image. "Most likely it has hair on it. He used hair follicles for the DNA test. It's a sample of Don's hair obtained when he got his hair trimmed. He had on that t-shirt..." I stopped cold, remembering I was divulging confidential information Trenton had provided in therapy. I had intended to provide just enough general information for Tina to guide her to what she would be looking for. She didn't need to know about the hair cut. "Be careful not to shake it out or anything." I instructed.

"Well, hell, if we need Don's hair, maybe Jess still has some hanging around in a bed sheet or towel…"

"Tina, come on." I appreciated her reluctance but knew she could pull it off. It was uncharacteristically shy of her not to take up an adventure.

"I'm just messing with you. Maybe I can get a quickie in with one of the trainers when I'm in the locker room."

"Tina!" She knew exactly how to throw me a curve ball and make me blush just by the mention of sexual prowess. "I'll be waiting for your call."

I sat in silence, wishing I had thought to tell Tina to call me and utilize Face Time so that I could literally see what she was doing. That probably was not a good idea and would really draw even more suspicion. Suspicion. I wondered why Tina was so suspicious of Don. Everyone else was apparently in love with him—Jessica, Rachel, Trenton, even Jamal considered him a friend. After all, from what I guessed, he wasn't a dirty gambler. From what I could pull from Jess without appearing that I was diagnosing him, he was into the Internet and those gambling machines. There couldn't be that many gambling casinos in Atlanta. At least not as many as Atlantic City. That didn't preclude that he didn't travel. It wasn't like he was a personality gambler or did anything illegal like fixing horse or car races. He might have been just a social gambler gone awry. Maybe dabbled in a little sports betting.

The first car since I had been sitting there for what had to be over five minutes pulled into the lot, parking directly next to Tina's despite the fact that the lot was almost completely empty. I wondered what the guy did for a living that he came to work out in the middle of the day. It made me think that maybe Tina didn't like Don because he didn't have a strong work ethic. Tina said he never seemed to be at work and often was with Jessica for a late breakfast before she went to the station to broadcast the news at noon. I just think he had a flexible work schedule. Tina should understand that. She worked flexible hours and no one could accuse her of being lazy.

No, Tina just didn't like him because Jess became all docile around him and spent so much time pumping him up. Or maybe it was simply because he messed up her money. Not that Jess was a financial wizard. She always made a lot of money and she always spent a lot of money. Money would burn a hole in her pocket, as my mom would say.

I reached for my purse to check to see if I had enough cash for airport parking when I arrived back in Cleveland and remembered that Tina had taken my purse. Curious, I surveyed Tina's purse. We used to do a scavenger hunt team-building exercise in graduate school where you had to find everything on the list among your personal belongings. Tina would be a prized player; her purse had everything but the kitchen sink. Several pages from a Wells Fargo Bank Statement were not so neatly folded in the middle pocket visible from a cursory glance. I don't know if it was the anxiety of waiting and needing the distraction, but I impulsively pulled it out. The printed copy of the online account was in the name of Jessica Davis, several check numbers were highlighted in yellow and the description read Ubold Holdings, each amount in the thousands. I quickly began adding the total only to have the mental list disappear when the phone rang.

I was sure Tina could hear my heart pounding through the phone. Each minute she had been in there dissolved my certainty that this was a good idea and heightened my assuredness of the risk we were taking. Did Tina and Jess realize that Ubold Holdings was owned by the Tucker family and headed up by Jamal? Were the payments being made by Jessica on Don's behalf? I would have to find a way to get this information from them without Tina getting angry at me for snooping in her purse. The act was really just an anxiety buster. How was I to know that there was valuable information that maybe even they didn't realize was valuable?

"Okay, Sister Nun, after waiting for the front desk guy to get off the phone with some crazed member who left an expensive watch in the shower room, I practically had to promise to sleep with the dude. He finally let me go into the gym after I told him I needed to secretly check out if my husband was here instead of on the business trip that he claimed he was on. I really got his sympathy when I told him that he was sneaking around with his mistress that he kept on the other side of town in some high priced condo..." Tina's voice began to rise with anger as she thought about the gall of her imaginary soon-to-be-ex-husband. "He either felt sorry for me or was like 'this is way too much information and I ain't gonna get up in all this drama.' So he just waved his hand like 'let this nutty lady just stop talking to me'...Oh, here's the locker room. Okay," she began to whisper, "There doesn't seem to be anyone in here. Oh, I can hear the shower going. I can't talk. If you don't hear or see me in ten minutes, come in and get my butt out of here."

Digging around in Tina's purse only heightened my anxiety. Tina had left the key in the ignition, and I turned the key to allow the radio to distract me. If Atlanta had an easy listening channel it wouldn't be pre-set on Tina's dial. She had her iPod attached to the system, so I would have to fiddle with the controls to get the radio function. The script that ran across the screen read "No Lie 2 Chainz" as the pulsating beat of Tina's unrecognizable playlist filled the interior of the SUV. Within seconds the music made me even more anxious, and I quickly turned it off and began to hum the first gospel song that would come to my mind. In the middle of humming Brian Courtney Wilson's "Already Here," a loud tap on the window brought out a primal scream.

"Tina, you crazy woman! You scared me half to death." Tina laughed with the joy from having intentionally thrown me off balance so easily as she pulled out a corner of a white t-shirt from my purse.

"Oh, my God! Get in the car. You got it!" I was giddy with

excitement. We were two steps closer to getting Jessica exonerated in under an hour's time. Well, maybe.

"I am good. I am goooood." Tina jumped into the front seat and turned the ignition, filling the car again with the sounds of 2 Chainz. "Sister Nun, I didn't know you were into Chainz and my man Drake. I actually designed one of his houses."

"I just had it on for a second as a distraction waiting for you. Turn it off now so I can hear how you managed to pull this off."

I am sure Tina embellished a bit how she deftly scanned the rows for locker 911 and then used the makeshift lock combination opener we had made from a pop can. She was actually surprised that it worked so easily, but from her narrative it sounded like it was more to her great skill and competency than the information and direction provided over the phone by Tony Labella on how to pick a lock. Following his instructions, within a half hour we had cut out a device from a Diet Coke can with just a magic marker and scissors. Inserting the metal shim into the combination lock quickly released the handle. With our homemade device, Tina had mastered opening two of the best brands of combination locks in under thirty seconds. If this break and entry didn't work, there would even be more hell for me to pay. Either way she was doomed. If she got caught, she was going to get arrested, for real this time. If she didn't get caught, she had agreed to go to a movie with Tony. It wasn't my fault that she made that promise in order not to have the call appear like she was totally using him.

To our great surprise and my even greater relief, the t-shirt was there; just as Trenton had described where he kept it—safe in his gym locker in case he ever needed to confront his mother with evidence. I was not at all sure what we were going to do next with this information, but just as it led Trenton to clarity about which one of his parents might be involved with the death of Don Davenport, it would surely lead us to that same confirmation.

"We should find a plastic bag to keep it in so that it doesn't get all contaminated in your suitcase. You know, just like in *Law & Order* where they have all the evidence in plastic bags." Tina and I shared an affinity for the television show and loved when the cable networks ran a *Law & Order* marathon. We were feeling pretty good about our detective work on behalf of our dear sister friend. I only wish we could tell her about our lead, but our excitement might be a bit premature.

My flight was scheduled to leave at six that evening which meant we had just about enough time to stop by Jessica's condo and give her a quick hug, get back to Tina's to gather my things, and stop to get something to eat on the way to the airport.

"How about some Chinese?" Tina suggested as our food option. "It will be quick, and I know a great place on the way to the airport." I quickly agreed. Within twenty minutes we were seated across from each other in a pink and black booth at Grand China Restaurant waiting for our orders of General Tso chicken and shrimp fried rice when a muscular white guy scooted into the booth next to Tina. Tina was taken aback but not scared by the familiarity. I guessed him to be one of the many, many acquaintances Tina knew in Atlanta.

"Hey, lovely ladies, mind if I join you for a second? I'm waiting for my take-out order." Tina had a way of attracting all types of men, but I didn't really think this would be her type at all. His rough face with grooves like a peach stone made him appear a lot older than he might actually be. He was definitely a biker kind of guy while Tina's taste was more of a luxury vehicle.

"Uh, do I know you from somewhere? You're mighty bold not waiting for an answer to whether we wanted your company or not." Tina's tone was inviting although she clearly got her message across.

"Well, like I said, it will just be a minute. Couldn't resist a pretty face and just feeling a little protective."

"Ouch," Tina cried in pain. She wasn't pretending. "Stop, take your hand off me." Tears were instantly coming down her face. In an instant, I lunged across the booth, only to have the large fist of his right hand quickly grip my open palm that was positioned to slap him across his face.

"Don't you dare scream and I won't hurt either of you." I sat back on the leather seat in robot fashion locking eyes with Tina whose fear mirrored mine.

"Just like I said, just want to deliver a message. You stay out of trying to discover anything about Don Davenport's death, and your friend Jessica will be just fine. You hear me. You stay out of this." Tina's tears turned to anger as she began to rub her leg upon the release of his grip and began muttering obscenities in an almost audible tone as if she intentionally wanted him to hear her. I sat in shocked disbelief. And just as quickly as he slipped into the booth, he slipped out of it.

"You lovely ladies have a nice day." He nodded and disappeared.

CHAPTER 18

I felt a tad guilty when Joy thanked me for going over and beyond the call of duty with treating and taking care of Trenton. My ability to concentrate in our last session was seriously compromised by the paralyzing fear we experienced by the man Tina now dubbed Big Hand as she continued to nurse the massive bruise on her right thigh. Resembling the fervor and resolve of pre-teen lovers vowing to stay together for the rest of their lives, we swore never to breathe a word about our "royal encounter" which was our code word for the incident in the Chinese restaurant. We were fearful that our phone conversations might even be tapped.

I had not breathed a word to Jon or even to Randy under the guise of confession which was typically how I shared confidential or sensitive information with him. I wanted to destroy the t-shirt, but Tina insisted on keeping it in a safe place that she would not reveal even to me. She wasn't about to allow Big Hand to scare her out of possessing a key piece of evidence that she masterfully secured even if we never had an opportunity to discover anything through its contents.

"Trenton actually seems to be getting some benefit from this therapy thing you've got going on and actually even likes you." Gratefully, Joy had shifted the topic to what was going on with her family after receiving reassurance that things were okay in Atlanta with Jessica and Tina. She appeared to be either unaware of any alleged connections between Don Davenport's death and her family or impartial to any possible connection. She asked about Jess as she would any of my sisters, was content knowing that Tina was not in jail and not considered a suspect, and was especially relieved that Jessica was managing as best as could be expected under the circumstances. I appreciated that Joy seemed genuinely interested in Jessica's welfare and routinely asked for details even if it was in a somewhat business-like manner. Compassionate empathy had never been Joy's forte although she tirelessly worked toward positive outcomes for those individuals and causes she cared about.

Her assessment of the positive results of Trenton's therapy was relayed in a similar tone, although with Trenton a trace of fondness peppered the conversation. "He seems to have grown up through his parent's separation, if you want to call it that. It's more like Rachel's pouting and needing even more attention has been disguised as this so-called marital separation. How someone who requires more attention than a newborn manages to actually find ways to get even more attention is beyond me. Anyway, Trenton seems to be a bit more at peace. Not about the gay thing. He's always been self-assured there, thank God, but more like things are okay and the family is back together again. It's weird, but in this family I will settle for weird as our normal."

"I'm glad to hear that he is doing okay. He's making real progress." Actually we still had not talked about his sexual orientation and anything that I was contracted to explore with him. "I look forward to seeing him." That wasn't a lie. As frightening as it was to possess any information concerning Don's death that might lead to one of the Nelsons, it was equally as unsettling to know that Jessica could be framed for something as serious as murder.

As the weeks since the investigation turned to months, Jessica spent hours reading, journaling, and meditating under Tina's careful watch. Tina even read all Jess's letters, emails, and Facebook postings and tweets, deleting anything negative before Jessica was allowed to read them. Since returning from Atlanta, my anxiety heightened with the prospect of learning more from Trenton despite the fact that we were forcibly admonished not to follow up on any information that could serve to clear Jessica. With every session Trenton felt compelled to take me on his journey, unraveling family secrets along the way. Each session brought us closer to the truth behind Don Davenport's death.

One day, Trenton arrived uncharacteristically late. It was less than five minutes, but I had already begun to worry that he had been freaked out about telling me about the evidence for a paternity test that was now somewhere in Tina's possession. Maybe Big Hand had gotten to him as well.

"Sorry to be late, Dr. Carpenter. Mom had the car, and even though I told her the appointment was for three o'clock and not three-thirty, she got home at 2:55 and tried to convince me that I could make it uptown in just fifteen minutes with time to spare well before the fifteen-minute acceptable range for being late for a therapy session was up." I smiled. "You probably know that she operates by her own time zone." I gave a soft chuckle in reply.

The everyday khaki pants he wore were definitely not from the discount chain Old Navy; well-tailored and form–fitting, they most likely cost three times as much as any pair in that store. He sat and neatly folded his hands on the cotton gabardine.

"How are you today?" Trenton was consistently polite.

"Thanks for asking... as you always do. And I am happy to report that I am fine." I really liked Trenton. With a reasonable degree of certainty, I believed that he was the individual Tony Labella described as the guy who visited Don before his death. I was equally convinced that there was a simple, honorable explanation for his encounter with Don that day, but I also had a hunch that if his explanation didn't implicate him, it implicated someone he needed and wanted to protect. When given the chance to do our own DNA testing with hair follicles from the t-shirt, we might discover what could have motivated someone from the Nelson family to permanently silence Don. I couldn't rule out Trenton, but it was hard to think about him as the responsible party. Was he the reason for Don's expenditures and why Jessica would have made the checks out to his father's company to repay some kind of loan? I wasn't quite sure how to manage this session. Trenton usually took the lead, but today not only was he uncharacteristically late, but he wasn't continuing his life story as he had previously done from session to session.

"In the previous session, you were telling me how you manage your mother's obsession, I think that is how you referred to it, about Don being your biological father." I tried my best to reflect his words so as to veil my curiosity. I felt the need to know if what he knew would help Jessica. The thought sparked a twinge of guilt that I was exploiting a patient for a self-serving agenda. I would cross that bridge after his secret was revealed.

"I remember. I just not sure that it's important anymore. After all, Uncle Don is dead and it wouldn't serve anybody any good to take us down that path. Mom and Dad are back in their groove, however crazy that groove may be. Dad's paid more attention to her as a result of her leaving and Uncle Don dying. A little attention goes a long way with Mom." He settled back in the leather bucket chair handing over the session to me. I was dumbfounded. Personally, I wanted to probe more to discover if there was motive in the revelation of his paternity; professionally I knew that I shouldn't.

"Uh…but this isn't really about your mom. It is about you. Are you content without having confirmation?" I sorta went halfway between the personal and professional.

"I'm okay."

"But you spent so much time and energy thinking through how to obtain that DNA sample and most likely have invested dollars to getting a test done." Now I was clearly in the category of personal. Where was Maury Povich when you needed him?

"The money doesn't matter."

"Oh…oh…" I could almost feel Big Hand choking me.

"It's okay, really."

"Okay, okay." I was trying to find my voice. "I respect your decision and your maturity. I would certainly be curious." I was so far off the psychologist track. My curiosity had nothing to do with serving Trenton's interest.

"There's a lot at stake here, Dr. Carpenter. My family…the family that I know needs to stay together. Not just because of the inheritance dollars." He paused to check out whether or not this was new information to me.

"I assume Auntie Joyce told you the conditions of the inheritance. That's why I am here, right…you are supposed to turn the gay away. Mom and Dad are to stay married, Dad has to stay at Ubold and Auntie Joyce has to stay locked up." His paraphrase of the convent was said with a sly smile.

I nodded as he continued.

"It's funny. Grandpa controls us from the grave, and now Uncle Don does too."

CHAPTER 19

Regina Academy's Casino Night, held annually in early fall, had morphed over the last twenty years from your basic high school scholarship fundraiser to one of the city's major social events. It was the event where women formerly known as high school nerds introduced themselves to their former classmates as presidents of one of Ohio's Fortune 500 companies.

Formerly chubby adolescents, who appeared even less attractive in grey and red pleated uniform skirts, returned to their alma mater to enjoy the jaw-dropping reactions as former classmates examined their model figures. Those who had moved up several socioeconomic levels through marriage made sure to impress others by bidding on the most expensive live auction items of the evening. The vast majority of the thousands of alumni of the formerly all-girls Catholic high school and their family and friends came to the event because it was the place to be and be seen. This adult event rated very high on the fun meter and tickets sold out quickly.

"It doesn't feel right to be all dressed up when it's practically in the middle of the afternoon for me. I slept until eleven o'clock this morning, longer than Wayne. But, hey, I'm awake now." My sister Dana tugged at her animal print pencil skirt allowing the hem to reach slightly above the knee. Her excitement for getting this party started was evident in her gait.

I had not been back to Regina Academy Casino Night since my early years of leaving the convent. That evening was a disastrous date with a recently divorced recovering alcoholic who, within a half hour after arriving, got into a verbal fight with one of the security guards whom he suspected had slept with his ex-wife. Coming tonight with Jon on a double date with Dana and Darien would erase all possibility of any post-traumatic stress occurring from recalling that experience.

"You'll be grateful not to have to get on the shuttle to get your car at the end of the night." Jon replied as Dana and Darien turned to greet their neighbors and the excitement of the evening began. As always, engineering the best parking options for large scale events was part of Jon's pre-planning. Others must have had arriving early on their to-do list as well, for there was already a sizable crowd entering the school gym that had been transformed into a gaming room with slot machines lining the floor so that the excited cries could be heard from winners at the more loose machines strategically placed in the middle.

Within an hour of the start time, the building had reached

capacity. First floor classrooms were filled with table players, the New Orleans-style buffet dinner was being enjoyed by diners seated at tables positioned at the entrance of the cafeteria, and dancing had begun at the far end.

"You can tell the folks here who are serious gamblers. Despite the fact that there is no real money being won, people are losing their minds at those tables." Darien placed his plate at the table next to Jon. "I took a walk through the classrooms; the people were looking at me when I entered like I was causing them to lose their home if I distracted them."

"There are some pretty decent prizes I hear." I couldn't exactly remember what the invitation stated, but I was impressed.

"Top prize is a vacation package to Vegas for four which is motivating a lot of these folks, including me. And even the small prizes are worth getting some serious game on." Dana said.

"It's good to have people enjoy themselves for a good cause. A real party with a purpose," Jon chimed in.

"Well, I'm getting back to winning." Dana rose and Darien joined her. Jon spotted the head of the speech department from the university and had made a bee-line to catch up with him just as Joy approached the table.

"Nice crowd, huh, I almost didn't find you." Joy had told me that she would "make an appearance" at the event. We had hoped to see each other.

"Now this is a fundraiser that is actually fun. Beats any

sit-down, boring chicken dinner with a bunch of speeches honoring donors."

"Hey, are you criticizing my hospital's honored tradition?" Joy quickly retorted.

I grimaced. "I really wasn't talking about that one specifically, but now that you mention it..."

"I'm agreeing with you. I have to drag folks and bribe them to come. Not the case here. In fact, I have some of our donors in the big ballers' room that I have to go say hello to. Why don't you come with me?" Joy gestured for me to get up and follow her to the second floor.

"You're kidding me? There's actually a private room for big ballers?"

"Well, not exactly private. It was publicized on your ticket invitation. For a mere five thousand dollars you get to play in the faculty lounge, have a few "free" drinks, fancy hors d'oeuvres and the opportunity to win even more vouchers for prizes that the people in this room probably already donated to the fine nun's academy." We headed up the back stairway to the second floor and made our way down the dimly lit hallway.

"Actually it is a great opportunity for the business leaders to meet. I don't have any problem getting them to buy a ticket. By now, the tickets are coveted."

We entered the spacious room where I recalled as a student being enamored with the mystery of what was behind its forbidden doors. As a teacher here, I remembered putting the final details on lesson plans and talking about troubled students with other faculty. It was a bit surreal to enter the same space that had been transformed to rival any of the swankiest suites in big table gaming.

"Oh, geez, watch your language, guys. The nuns are here." Kevin LaCasa, one of the city's largest developers, shouted as laughter rippled through the space. It was ironic that anyone would warn others to clean up their language in the presence of Joy whose language was frequently peppered with obscenities. She made her way around the table planting soft kisses and warm handshakes among the men. I matched faces to the names I had read in the newspaper's business section as Joy made her rounds introducing me to men who were her peers.

"Many of these men knew my dad pretty well, and a lot of them are where they are because he gave someone the nod for them to get the position they have." We both scanned the room as we found two lounge chairs nestled in the corner. There were only a few women in the room besides us, and, apart from their clothing and makeup, their behaviors would go undetected as anything unique.

"There is a different energy in the room. You can almost grab the air—it is so thick with power and influence," I said. Joy gave a weak smile as if the energy had physically forced her lips to move upward.

"You're right. It's an energy I am very familiar with, and thankfully, I only have to enter into it on my choosing these days." She thoughtfully swirled the Merlot in the glass.

"We've just about worked out all of the last details of

executing the will; the Nelsons will be headed back to Atlanta as one happy family next week, and I can get back to worrying more about the cost of care for the uninsured and other more important topics." Joy looked down and studied the glass as if to wonder what happened to all the wine that was in there just a few seconds ago. I was glad that she didn't notice my shock and confusion. I was certain that Rachel and Trenton both had scheduled appointments for the next two weeks. Obviously, Joy rightfully assumed that I had accurate information on her family members that were my patients, but that clearly wasn't the case.

"Uh…I'm surprised the Nelsons aren't here tonight." I fumbled my way to a response.

"You're kidding, right? Rachel, with your help of course, has finally admitted that she has a problem and prided herself in not even having an itch to engage in even fake gambling tonight. In celebration, they're having a family movie and pizza night instead."

"I take no credit for any improvement in that arena." I honestly claimed. This was the first mention of any gambling problem that I had heard.

"Well, you know that she has transferred that habit into shopping, but that, we can handle. You can always return a pair of Jimmy Choo shoes. We couldn't do that when she was turning tables. I was really worried. She's lucky she wasn't the one falling from a balcony or committing suicide or faking her death that night."

Placing my wine glass firmly on the table, I didn't know if I was woozy from its content or what I was hearing. I gave Joy a blank stare. Was she implying that Don might have committed suicide or faked his death?

"I know you can't talk about what you hear in therapy and I respect that…" she said in a mocking tone, "…sort of." A blonde female server clad in a bright blue tailored shirt, matching tie, and black pants approached and began refilling Joy's glass.

"You're drinking Riesling, right? I'll be back with that." She quickly turned away.

"Anyway, I am eternally grateful to you for taking care of Rach and Trenton. And indirectly, you took care of Jamal as well. Randy helped Jamal keep it together too. You both came back in my life when I really needed you." I had no choice but to take this all in and then sort it out later.

"You know, things do happen for a reason and sadly, although Don's gone, it's a relief on so many accounts. He's now at peace; Rachel can keep her problem in control and whatever secrets they shared can stay buried; Jamal doesn't have to worry about Don influencing Trenton to live a life as confused as apparently his was, and the business will be on track financially. And most importantly, I no longer have to be one of the cast members in that nightmare of a reality show that has been my life for the past two years."

Joy misread my confusion for anger.

"Oh, I'm sorry. I didn't mean to be so insensitive. Jessica

will be okay. It will work out for her as well. I'm sorry that she even had to be a part of this mess." The blonde server eased her way between us and excused herself for reaching over as she poured Riesling into my glass.

"You know that God always takes care, Kath. She won't be down for much longer." Joy stated definitively.

Not knowing what to think, I took a big gulp of wine in response.

CHAPTER 20

The heat of the sun made it possible to still go sleeveless and to wear shorts. Living in Cleveland, one took advantage of any day where the sun was bold enough to shine, especially in September. As a result, Randy and I moved out to the patio to eat a late lunch. Having Randy over at my house on a Sunday afternoon was a rare occurrence. After a weekend of weddings, Masses, and the occasional funeral, he treasured a good nap in front of the television and over-indulging on Doritos and Diet Pepsi during the football game. My Sunday afternoons were dedicated to writing, as the publisher's deadline for the next *You and Your Partner* book loomed on the horizon. A sleepless night of playing over and over again the conversation with Joy prompted this unplanned meeting with Randy. I trusted that Randy would appreciate the necessary interruption to his afternoon once he heard the details of my conversation with Joy.

"I need to ask you something about Jamal." Randy was tearing through the croissant and piling the chicken from the pasta salad on the bread. It was a bit of a girly lunch, but I had all the ingredients and could put it together easily. "Did he talk to you about Rachel having a gambling problem?"

Randy paused. "Is this confessional material?" He asked. "I thought Rachel was your patient? Am I supposed to talk about what I know about her to you?" He paused, placing the sandwich on the plate.

"Well, I guess she is your patient and not mine, and what I know was more told to me in the confidence of friendship, but it doesn't matter anyway because the answer is no. Did Rachel have a gambling habit?"

"Really? Jamal never mentioned anything. And, no, I guess this does not need to be in confession or even in a therapy session for that matter…" Randy and I had exchanged confidential information over the years by signaling that I was "going to confession" if it was something I needed to share with him or "becoming a patient" if it was something he needed me to know. Randy appeared confused by my response. I continued.

"Apparently the Nelsons are returning to Atlanta as an intact family next week, and Joy is selling the Bratenahl home. I checked my schedule and sure enough, sessions have been canceled. However, they are still patients so I just need you to answer my questions rather than ask any if you would be so obliging."

"They're going to try to sell that house in this economy?

It was already the highest-priced home in Cleveland. I mean it is fabulous and all. Right on the lake…"

"Wrong focus, Randy," I laughed and redirected his thoughts. "The Nelson family was falling apart and suddenly now they are all back together with Don conveniently out of the picture and Jessica on the hook. Did you know that Jamal and Rachel had resolved their issues?"

"I guess it depends on what issue you are asking they resolved. I only know that Jamal thought his wife was having a hard time with the death of their long-time friend and he was committed to trying to spend more time with her moving forward, especially now that Trenton was away at college." Randy pulled open the bag of Kettle Backyard Barbecue potato chips and stuffed a handful in his mouth.

"It was that simple?" I asked. Men had a way of simplifying issues like relationships that were really complex and taking things that were simple like managing household chores and making them complex.

"I think it was. He seemed to understand that he had a wife who was high maintenance and knew with time that she would settle down after she stopped grieving about not having a running buddy with Don. He was concerned about the impact on Trenton, and he was more concerned about some business transactions that he needed to get cleared up before an audit."

"So, he was aware that they spent a lot of time together?"

"Of course," Randy said implying that it was a silly question.

"Then he must have been aware of her feelings for Don."

"Uh…if there were 'feelings,' he wasn't worried about them, and really his wife should have known as well that her feelings were misplaced. They've all known each other since high school."

"I'm not following." I lifted a fork full of chicken pasta salad to my mouth more as a response to my anxiety than an attempt to manage hunger.

"What's there to follow? It's the same reason that Jessica finally broke up with Don. Hey, I didn't really know the guy, but everyone who really did know him knew that the gambling was a diversion, an emotional release of anxiety. Jamal says it was a pattern. When he couldn't quite fully commit to any woman and wasn't man enough to let his emotions take him to the other side, he got involved with gambling."

"So Jamal's concern was more that he would influence Trenton?" I recalled Trenton saying that Uncle Don had a lot of fun in the clubs.

"Jamal wanted Trenton to be secure in his orientation. He knew how tormented Don was all of his life trying not to be who he really was, and Jamal didn't want that kind of a life for his son. He would rather have a happy gay son than a confused, suicidal, heterosexual one. He didn't want Don trying to influence Trenton with his lifestyle choice mumbo jumbo."

I sat in silence trying to put it all together while managing my emotions about the lies that Rachel had spewed to me over the course of many sessions. But maybe they weren't lies? And if they weren't lies, how did they represent her truth?

Randy took a long swig of Diet Pepsi and crumbled the napkin by his plate on the patio table. "I don't know if this helped or confused you more." Silence was a rare response from me.

"Just trying to put it all together, that's all. Jamal was really upset about Don's death, I know."

"He was. You know how it goes. People go back to their last conversation with the deceased, and his was not a good one. He argued with him almost to the point of a physical fight. He was mad at him for messing up on the job and pretty angry that Don's influence was damaging Trenton and getting him mixed up in his crap."

"I don't know about that." I quickly thought it through a bit. "My understanding was that Don was really following Trenton's lead and socializing at clubs that were Trenton's choice. You didn't hear that from me." I quickly added.

"Well, money was disappearing pretty fast. Don claimed he was bankrolling Rachel. Rachel was doing her share of shopping, but she claimed the larger amounts of money were going to Trenton. Jamal, playing armchair psychologist, always believed that Don used gambling as a way for a quick thrill that he needed to mask his issues around not resolving his sexual orientation. Jamal accused Don of introducing

Rachel to the thrill of gambling and messing up his family by pulling Trenton into all of it."

"That could be true. It's just like any other addiction that people use to mask emotional issues." I couldn't resist the psychological commentary. "And it makes sense that Don would project his manner of resolution for his own sexual orientation onto Trenton."

"Yeah, well it got Jamal pretty angry that he was messing with his family. That's Jamal's only son, and he saw his buddy going downhill and ruining his life and he didn't want him taking his wife and son down with him. He was pretty messed up when we were in Atlanta and pretty scared about everything falling apart: his marriage, his family, and the business. It took me some time to get him to a decent place emotionally before I could leave. I almost had to call you."

"Wait, you saw Jamal while we were in Atlanta?"

"Oops... I forgot I didn't let you know that." He stopped as if to ponder how he could forget such an important fact. I wondered about that as well. "At the same time you were headed to Atlanta to help Tina, Jamal called and he was a mess. I asked him to hang on until I could get there, and I would get to see him."

I gave him a quizzical look.

"I didn't want to tell you and make it seem like supporting Tina and Jessica wasn't a priority. Jamal's been reaching out to me and you start feeling sorry for the guy. He's carrying a heavy load with some huge business crisis that he was trying to handle confidentially so that it wouldn't leak to the press or stakeholders and really plummet the business. He was just about to fire Don and was trying to do it while still protecting his family and the business when he ended up dead."

"Wow," I gasped.

"Obviously Rachel and Trenton were pretty close to Don. Jamal's had his head in the sand about a lot of things. When he emerged, his world was falling apart—his wife was having a breakdown, his son was being influenced by his friend in ways that he could have easily prevented if he was being a real father, and it was all happening in the midst of a business crisis that he barely knew anything about. He was pretty angry with Don before he died."

"Was he angry to the point that he might have accidently killed him?" The question appeared to come out of the blue. But didn't Tony Labella say that there must have been some kind of physical fight before his plunge?

Randy put down the chip that was about to enter his mouth. "He's certainly feeling guilty enough as if he had killed somebody."

CHAPTER 21

When I arrived at the office on Monday, Connie smiled a good morning and directed my attention to the large fall floral bouquet on the desk. The burst of orange was a sharp contrast to the beige countertop.

"Wow! They're lovely but they look like a funeral arrangement. Somebody die?"

"Well, sorta. They're a thank you from the Nelsons. They regret that they had to return to Atlanta in time for Trenton to get back to school. They both cancelled this week's appointments."

"That's nice that they remembered you." A bit of sarcasm crept into my tone.

"Oh, these are for you." Connie smirked. "But they did remember me as well, except I got a nice fat American Express gift card. Obviously, not the appropriate gift for you, as Rachel told me when she called, but she certainly hoped that I would accept the card as their gift of gratitude. I let her know that it was only in that spirit that I would accept such a gift."

I looked at her dubiously, trying to recall if a gift card was the first of its kind thank you that we had received. Try as I might to discourage such a practice by always citing the fact that they had really done the work, some patients just needed to put closure to their therapy experience with a gift.

"Well, you enjoy your shopping spree, Connie. My flowers are lovely, but if you don't mind, I'll keep them up front until I am ready to leave. They will be perfect in the foyer at home. I'll enjoy them there."

I started to head down the hallway when Connie summoned me back to the front desk.

"Wait! There are notes here for you that were delivered with the flowers." She handed me the small florist card and a standard-sized envelope, both with "Dr. Carpenter" written on the front.

"Okay, thanks." I said, grabbing them and instinctively tearing open the small card as I walked down the hallway. Rachel's handwriting matched her personality with lavish loops and swirls. She used two cards to write out her message:

Dr. K.,

Sorry that we could not see you before we left. Thanks for making me whole again.

Will stop in when we come to Cleveland and you be sure to holler at us if you ever come to Atlanta.

Love,
Rachel

What did being whole mean for her? If she had a gambling problem, was the problem solved? There was absolutely no reason that I could think of for Joy to claim her sister had a gambling problem, if it wasn't true. Was she over her phantom love affair with Don? Or was the love affair with gambling as a result of an emotional connection with Don and their shared addiction? As Randy pointed out, being as close to Don as she and Jamal had been, it would have been impossible for her not to know of Don's struggle with his sexual orientation.

Reaching my office, I pulled out Rachel's file. Writing case notes after a session with Rachel always proved challenging given the rambling nature of her narratives. But maybe there was a clue somewhere in her grieving that she was either involved or knew that Jamal was involved in Don's death. Trenton had clearly alluded to the fact. When he tried to confirm the paternity of his biological father, he was thwarted by his parents. Were they afraid that family secrets would be revealed? Would it disinherit them from their fortune? Didn't Joy say that her father still controlled them from the grave? Trenton had decided it was best not to open Pandora's Box to disconfirm his mother's claims. Tina and I would certainly agree there was something foreboding in that discovery, given our encounter with Big Hand.

The first few pages of case notes proved to be unenlightening. As the ringing phone signaled a patient was waiting in the front lobby, I tossed Rachel's file on the desk along with the letter from Trenton. I needed to focus for the long day of back-to-back patients.

By six o'clock I was exhausted but had managed to make it through sessions with a depressed middle-aged man whose life revolved around his now-limited activities with The Boy Scouts, who had banned him from volunteering on the suspicion that he was gay; an elementary school principal's codependency with her alcoholic husband; a business executive whose anxiety heightened with every reduction in the workforce; a young woman who was being seduced by her boyfriend's father; a nun contemplating leaving religious life to begin a relationship with the parent of one of her students; and a single mom overwhelmed with having to police her twin teenage daughters after finding them home with their boyfriends when she came home sick from work one day. With the work of unraveling the issues of these cases, there was no chance to slide in even a sideways thought about the Nelsons.

An emergency session came at the end of the day with Gladys Trout, the mother of a former student and patient. Gladys just needed to grieve on the anniversary of her daughter's death. Thinking about Chanelle and her tragic accidental death from a drug overdose left no room to perseverate about the Nelsons. It left me in a funky mood. After shedding a few tears with Gladys, I couldn't wait to get home to decompress with Jon.

"Tough day, I take it." Jon glanced at me as I walked into

the kitchen. He was alr
generous pieces with le
"Where's the cat that dragg

"It was a bit of a rough
came by the office. I didn't re
of Chanelle's death. Maybe that
ing all day."

Jon turned around and leaned … ping his hands on a linen dish towel. "I know … hard and probably will always be." He wrapped his long arms around my body and held tight until I could feel my breathing slowing and the muscles in my shoulders relaxing.

"I tell you what," Jon pulled back and looked me directly in the eyes; his own deep brown eyes could land him on any magazine's sexiest man alive list. "How about you go soak a bit in the Jacuzzi, and by that time dinner will be finished and then we can…" he paused for dramatic effect…"pop the DVD in and watch as many episodes of *Modern Family* as you can stand before you fall asleep."

As I made my way to the bedroom, I was already laughing.

CHAPTER 22

Jessica Davis was taken into custody on one of the warmest days in early October that Atlanta had experienced since 1976. Receiving the news from Tina only moments before it hit the six o'clock news in every major city made watching the segment appear to be like a recorded nightmare. She would continue to be featured as the lead story on every entertainment news magazine show that evening. Atlanta's once media darling was now its ratings magnet. Everyone was tuning in to witness the fall from grace. The cramping in my stomach was nowhere near a match for the pain that was evident in the expression on Jessica's face as she moved through the crowds to enter the courthouse. Despite attempts to hide from the camera, her face was a household presence in Atlanta, and the juxtaposition of her anchor glam shot and her demeanor walking into municipal court was striking. After months of investigation, Jessica was now being taken into custody to await trial for the murder of Don Davenport.

We lacked details of what actually turned the tables to move Jessica from suspect to accused. It was impossible to decipher what Tina was saying on the phone because she was beyond inconsolable. Her sobbing was guttural, the wailing piercing, and her breathing shallow.

In a daze I packed a few tops to rotate with my jeans and tossed in a black knit pantsuit that could serve for a professional look in case I needed it. Going through the motions of packing for the trip to Atlanta mimicked its uncertainty. What kind of wardrobe would one need for attempting to get a loved one out of jail?

Jon and I rode in silence to the airport, after deciding that I would go to support Jess and Tina and he would head south on Monday or Tuesday if necessary. Jon's lawyer friends who represented Jessica cautioned that there would not be much movement on the weekend. It seemed to be particularly cruel to arrest her on a Friday, knowing that it was certain to be at least a few nights in jail.

Tina arrived uncharacteristically early to pick me up at the airport. In fact, she was waiting in the terminal when I landed.

"I didn't know what to do until you got here so I just drove around, then parked and came in. I've had three almond croissants and a couple of low-fat muffins at Au Bon Pain waiting for you." Tina wrapped her arms around me and tightened the grip.

"What's the plan?" Looking directly into her eyes, I

confirmed that she was indeed in as bad a shape as I felt. I had never seen Tina in public without makeup, and her admission of eating so many carbohydrates non-stop was even scarier.

"I don't know. I don't know. I don't know." Tina's tears fell softly down her cheeks with each declaration of not knowing being less and less audible.

"Okay. Okay. I'm here now. We'll figure out something. Do you remember where you parked the car?" I asked. She nodded.

"Are you okay to drive? It might be easier if you drive instead of trying to tell me where to go." The steady stream of tears didn't stop.

"How about if I set the GPS and I drive to your condo, okay? We can figure out our next steps then." She nodded then changed her mind quickly. "No, we can go to the jail. We'll be able to see Jess. "

"Are you sure?"

"Cynthia's there and Tony called in a favor so we can see her. We're sorta her attorneys." I smiled. "Can't you get a degree online?" she humorously asked, letting me know that Tina was still kicking underneath the pain.

"Actually, I think you can get a degree to be a minister and end up officiating at your friend's wedding, but I don't think you can get a law degree to get a friend out of jail." Tina's respite was momentary and the tears began to roll again.

"She'll survive this weekend," I said, although the knot in my stomach defied that I really believed my words. "She will be out on Monday, for sure, once the judge can set bail." Again, my stomach turned, recalling that Jon had cautioned me to be prudent about when the case would come before the judge, and the fact that it was a murder charge made the release date unpredictable.

Tony Labella obviously had some juice for there were no questions asked as we waited to see Jessica. Cynthia, sensing that this was obviously not a happy time, rose to a level of professionalism that made the situation even more surreal.

Jessica's robotic walk to the table in the small visiting room left me breathless. Even with the added years, there was no possible resemblance to the former Miss Ohio Teen and second runner-up to Miss USA, physically or emotionally.

"Hey, at least there are no bars or glass that we have to place our hands on," Tina said, giving Jess a bear hug, and embracing her body that was at least ten pounds lighter than when I last saw her just a month ago. "And at least you don't have to wear that disgusting orange prison garb. Orange is not your color, girl. You would have had to insist on the blue ones." Tina straightened Jessica's oversize white shirt that practically reached the knees of her skinny jeans. I was glad to see the faint smile that came across her face.

"How are you doing, Jess?" I asked, leaning forward to give her a hug as well. She barely had the energy to hug back.

"I'm scared." She quickly gave voice to the fear that oozed out of her body.

"I know. I know. If you have to, you'll make it through the

night and you'll be out of here by morning." My attempt at a confidence builder was met with a flood of tears.

"I'll stay with you tonight. Cynthia will let me." Tina moved to hug her again.

"It might be a long stay," Jess released a depressed sigh.

"No more than two more nights at best. If your attorney can't pull strings and get you released tonight, then the worst case scenario is that you have the hearing on Monday and the case gets dismissed."

"Not likely." Jess definitively said. We both simultaneously shook our head.

"Not likely," she repeated, directly looking into Tina's eyes as if transmitting a signal.

"Oh, Jess, that is the depression talking. They have no evidence to reach probable cause. I know your attorneys are not supposed to talk, but they've told Jon that they're pretty confident that there isn't much of a case... just maybe some misinterpreted connections that they could clear up. Jess, can I ask, what did they mean by that?"

Silent tears flowed in a steady stream. Maybe I should not have been so direct.

"Oh, God, that stupid news poem!" Tina joined Jess with her tears.

"No, it's the checks. The checks. He had me make them out to Ubold."

I didn't know what to say next. Tina was now sobbing. Then she suddenly stopped short in an aha moment.

"Oh, God, Jess. Did you tell them? Did you tell them, Jess?" Incredulous, Tina stared at her. Jess gave her a blank stare in response.

"Damn it, Jess. Why?"

"I would have had to tell my attorneys, Tina. And besides, I didn't have to tell them." Tina shook her head in disbelief. I wondered what the hell was going on.

"They knew," she continued. Tina continued to shake her head with a soft murmur of no, no, no barely audible under her breath.

"There was a witness." Jessica declared. "And they found the note and they have the bank statements."

"Oh, shit. Oh, shit. Oh, shit." Tina began to pace the room.

CHAPTER 23

Tina pulled into the garage and parked way too close to her Escalade SUV which made it difficult for me to get out of the passenger side of the Mercedes sports car that she drove when she wasn't working at a design job. I wondered if it was intentional, as we had ridden back in silence after our visit with Jessica. Obviously, there was a lot of missing information that she and Jess had chosen not to share with me. I was feeling played by my biological sister and someone who I was strongly connected to as a sister, even if it was not biological. Tina, sensing my anger, waited me out. I didn't know where to start.

Careful not to ding the driver's door of the Escalade, I eased my way out of the fifteen inches or less that she left between the two vehicles. By the time I entered the loft, she had already thrown her Stella McCartney black tote on the counter and grabbed a bottle of wine from the fridge and began pouring a glass.

"You want to join me?" Her tone was so uncharacteristically

flat that I didn't recognize it as her voice. She didn't wait for a response and began pouring me a glass of Pinot Noir. I began drinking in silence, knowing that it would irritate Tina. From our childhood days, Tina was the pursuer in a fight, preferring to scream it out and get it over with so we could move on. I preferred the distance to stew, sulk, and ruminate and then deal with it at a later date. As adults, we both recognized all of the moves of the dance and were not proud of ourselves when we acted like this, but we were powerless to change the behavior. Maybe because the stakes were so high, tonight the energy shifted.

"Okay…what am I missing? Obviously Jess's situation is far worse than I know but hopefully not worse than I can imagine."

"She's innocent," Tina declared softly.

"I wasn't planning to doubt that at all, but why is she in custody?"

"Because…because…they have motive," Tina squirmed a bit.

"What? He owed her money? That wouldn't be unusual for someone who has a gambling habit to be in debt to someone they were once engaged to." It was a logical explanation, but we were no longer in the world of logic.

"They have physical evidence of a motive." Tina pulled out the counter-height lime-colored stool and sat with legs apart.

She must be referring to the bank statement that was

in Tina's purse when I was snooping, I thought. I remained silent.

"And now they can place her at the scene of the crime." Tina sighed. "We both have watched too many *Law & Order* episodes to know that it doesn't end well when you have that combination." This time I sighed with her.

"Details," I requested… rather, commanded.

Tina looked at me blankly.

"Damn it, Tina. I can't believe you and Jess have led me on like this. Jon has stuck his neck out getting her the best defense and we all have been supporting her and you're holding out valuable information. How long have you known this? I knew you were both holding on to something but didn't ever think in a million years that it was some serious mess like this. What is going on, Tina? Have you been afraid to tell me or have you been lying? Oh, my God, Tina. Have you been lying to me? That would be worse than the pain of the truth." My voice rose higher and higher until I was screaming and barely understandable.

The screaming served to place Tina in her comfort zone when she was feeling guilty. She felt she deserved to be screamed at and now she was ready to defend herself.

"I didn't know any of this… well, most of it until after I ended up getting arrested, or rather, put in jail. Jess was afraid I would keep doing stupid things to get her off the hook from being a suspect. She felt I needed to know so there wouldn't be two of us in deep trouble."

I began to shiver, and it wasn't because of the temperature. "Please tell me Jess wasn't responsible for the accident." I couldn't bring myself to call it a murder—if Jess was involved, it had to be an accident. The thought made me want to throw up. Tina just stared and I continued to probe.

"I get the motive thing. But she wasn't angry with him, more hurt. Even if she got so angry, she's so petite, I can't imagine her pushing someone so forcibly that it would actually cause harm, let alone kill someone. I can't believe this." Within seconds I managed somehow to settle myself on the overstuffed love seat, grateful that I hadn't fainted.

"It's not that bad. She didn't do it. She didn't kill him... even accidentally."

"Then what's the physical evidence they supposedly have?"

"If it's what we think it is, it shouldn't be too hard to clean up with good attorneys." She paused reflecting on her assessment.

"Continue." A soft churl reminded me that my stomach was still reacting to what I was hearing. I wanted her to confirm it was the checks. Jess had mentioned the checks.

"Jess thinks something that she did as a joke is now being taken as a death threat."

"What?"

"She interviewed this guy who wrote this best-selling book on how you could blackout words in a newspaper with a magic marker and create poems. He showed her how to do it on the show, and afterward, she created her own newspaper poem."

"And?" Tina was not making it easy to connect the dots.

"Well, the newspaper poem was about killing Don," I audibly cringed. "...but it was a joke," Tina quickly added. "She was thinking about Don as her 'anchor,' as the guy said was how you did it. You choose a topic or anchor, something you had a lot of emotion around, and then let the energy just guide you in crossing out words. It was real soon after she kicked him to the curb, so she was still heated. She started slashing words that turned into a poem about permanently slashing him. If you could call it a poem...Well, it was one of those newspaper poems, I guess."

"That sounds innocent enough. Certainly it was no proof that she actually killed him." This was sounding very bizarre, and if Jessica wasn't sitting in a holding cell at the moment, it would be laughable.

"I know that you are thinking it's laughable," Tina said as if to read my mind. "But it is the only thing we can come up with as something physical they would have as proof that she wanted to kill him."

"How would it come into evidence? Did they search her condo or the news studio?"

"No, they haven't searched her places. Somehow it ended up getting to Don."

"How does something end up getting to Don? She must have given it to him."

"Now don't freak out, Sister Nun." Tina moved a few steps back as if to avoid me jumping her. "I mailed it to him."

"You mailed it to him?" I echoed.

"I thought it was funny. How was I to know that he would end up dead and Jess in jail. I tried to fix it, which is how I got myself in jail." Tina noted my quizzing look. "Well, actually they wanted to ask me a few questions. Okay, I went to the detective and told him I wanted to confess."

"You confessed to killing Don? Tina!"

"No, silly. I'm not that stupid. I thought I could take the heat off Jess so I told them that I had sent the newspaper poem to him. I told the truth, but they still didn't believe me." She shrugged her shoulders. "I even showed them how it smelled like me. Well, like my perfume. I sprayed it a bit with Chanel No.5, the good stuff. Don would have known that it was me and not Jess who sent it 'cause she doesn't wear perfume. They have some policy at the newsroom because there so many folks with allergies."

"Oh, God, Tina," I sighed.

"No, it was a joke. I was mad at Don, too. Patrick and my boys started telling me that Don was finally coming out, and they saw him at the clubs a lot. I thought he was on the down-low or at least real confused. I saw him with a white woman, and then Patrick tells me he's hanging with the Children." Tina used Atlanta's nickname for gay men. "He's all caught up gambling and breaking Jessica's heart in little pieces."

"It is so crazy and sounds exactly like what you would do, but get back to how they are holding it against Jess now."

"Well, if I hadn't put a lie in there with the truth it may have been okay."

"Oyo Moia, Tina! Get to the point."

"I thought they would go in for it all as truth and it would help Jess out somehow. So, I told them I was driving her car that night."

"This is such a bad dream," I rubbed my forehead hoping it would ease the pending headache.

"I know. I know. It's not making sense. It will. You remember Jess left us that night to go home. Well, she ended up getting all nostalgic with us talking about our past loves and drove over to Don's condo. She actually saw him plunge to his death just as she arrived."

"Oh, God," I said and this time it was a prayer.

"Wait. It gets worse. I go the police station and tell this cop, who looks just like Guy Fieri with the spiked-up blonde hair on the Food Network channel, that I was driving Jessica's car that night and went over to see Don. He tells me that I am lying again. He doesn't believe I sent the newspaper poem or that I was driving Jess's car when I went to cuss Don out for hurting my best friend. But he puts me in a holding cell until they get proof that I'm really just plain crazy and not a criminal. I hang out with Cynthia and they come back about three in the morning to tell me to go home. They had a positive identification that it wasn't me in the car. Now I'm freaking out because I know for sure that they know Jess was there. So even though it was not my original intent, my plan worked. I got to find out how much they had on Jess even though I almost got myself arrested. At this point, I'm not sure if they have the newspaper poem, but I know they know Jess was there that night. She hadn't told them a thing about driving there that night when they questioned her."

"This is not good at all."

"Tell me about it. She was just scared and really thought no one saw her. At least that is what she told me on the phone that night." She hesitated. "But, you're not going to like this at all. I know I didn't like it all when Jess finally 'fessed up.'"

"She said they had a witness." I was able to connect the dots from our conversation when we visited Jess. No wonder Jessica was so scared, probably even more than we could ever imagine.

"I don't know how she thought she would be able to hide the fact. I think she actually went into the building and wasn't just sitting in her car as she first told me."

"It's not like Jess to lie. Why would she not tell you the truth? Why would she not tell us the truth?" My stomach did a double flip.

"She was… is petrified. Don had confessed to her that he had taken some funds to clear a gambling debt and just needed to have it back by the end of the month or something really lame like that. He had her make out a money order to Ubold and assured her he would handle the accounting and there would be no way to trace it back to her." My look of disbelief registered with her.

"It was denial," Tina quickly explained, "or codependency or whatever psychological term you guys put on it. Jess actually went for help, and that is what finally ended the relationship."

A deep sigh left my body. Poor Jess. A victim of the textbook behavior so many wonderfully talented women fall into under the guise of love. I shook my head in continued disbelief that this was happening in my life outside of my therapy practice.

"If she didn't tell anybody she was there maybe it would erase the fact that she was there. She didn't have enough confidence that if she told us the truth that we would believe her. She doesn't think anyone would believe she wasn't involved." Tina said sadly.

"She couldn't have done it." I said.

"She didn't do it." Tina affirmed.

CHAPTER 24

Tina and I descended the steps of Our Lady of Lourdes after ten-thirty Mass and although the sermon was inspiring and the music uplifting, we both avoided any fellowship and left in the same emotional state as we entered. Heavy on our minds and hearts was the reality that there was enough evidence to implicate Jessica and a high probability that the events might take a turn for the worse. We felt all "churched out" as in the lyrics of gospel singer Tamela Mann's "Take Me to the King." The words could not have been more appropriate. I was surprised that Tina had the popular gospel song downloaded on her iPod and thought it particularly providential that it had shuffled to the top and was now playing as we made our way over to the Atlanta police station. The trip was our last-ditch effort planned to cast doubt in another direction other than Jessica for who might have murdered Don Davenport.

Technically, Trenton Nelson was no longer an active patient. Denial was supporting me to keep the fact that I was acting on information gathered in the strictest of confidence—that of a patient-client relationship—in the back of my mind. Feeling literally like I was between a rock and a hard place with either exposing a patient or supporting a sister-friend, whom I believed was innocent, left me in a stupor. Acting on Tina's energy and plea to resurrect the t-shirt was the catalyst that got me to move.

We discussed the situation way into the wee hours of the morning and argued about the pros and cons of possibly taking a print from my "mystery" patient's intake papers and taking a hair follicle from the shirt and doing our own paternity test. Neither one of us knew if this was even possible, and with our only background in this area being television shows like *Law & Order* and *CSI*, our level of confidence that it could even be done and that it would yield accurate results was very low.

With the probability that sooner or later the police would unveil the truth of who sent the newspaper poem to Don, we hesitated to get Tony Labella involved anymore by asking him about the paternity test. We went round and round on possibilities. Tina was willing to be implicated in the crime believing that it would mess up the case so much that it was bound to create reasonable doubt about Jess's culpability. I reasoned that we would have just traded one mess for another. I could not imagine Tina surviving any jail time any more than I could Jessica. I had never revealed anything about Trenton's identity to Tina and reasoned that the risk of the police asking for the source was low enough. The stakes were high for getting Jess out of jail. We had to reveal the truth to move forward. We had no other choice.

We agreed the t-shirt must be a pretty important piece of evidence. After all, it had introduced us to Big Hand. If we turned it over to the police, it was bound to help Jessica in some way.

We had a plan for proof of our pure motivation to simply help Jessica. If we ended up being questioned by the police, or if we botched the t-shirt revelation, or worse yet, got apprehended again by Big Hand, Tina had not revealed where she kept the shirt, and I had not told her the identity of its owner. We had watched enough *Law & Order* shows to know that it is better not to know all of the details so one didn't have to feign ignorance. They would have to engage us both to get the full truth.

Tina arrived back to her loft after retrieving the evidence right before we went to Mass. There we prayed our butts off that what we were about to do would miraculously end this nightmare. We were now minutes away from the police station.

"I think I should start this off with the detective, especially if it turns out to be the same guy who questioned you before," I said as Tina hit replay on the car's radio dashboard so that we could again be comforted by the gospel song. We were taking what we hoped was a valuable piece of evidence to the police. It was helpful to imagine that it was our small offering being taken to the loving hands of a savior and king as the song implied. Or at least it would have to be my interpretation at the moment.

CHAPTER 25A

Tina sat erect with a posture I couldn't even remember witnessing in the forty-four years that she had been my sister. She resembled a school girl called into the principal's office, oddly quiet and already playing the part of the convicted.

Tina was right. The detective on the case did look like Guy Fieri on the Food Network channel, only his hair color didn't have the blonde streaks, and he definitely looked like he spent more time in the gym than the kitchen.

"Detective, thanks for seeing us. I'm Kathy Carpenter Hoffman and this is my sister, Tina." Detective Food Network Guy gave a coy smile and Tina immediately looked away. "We're here with some information on the Don Davenport murder," I continued, grateful that Tina was being cooperative and not talking.

"Oh, yes. I understand you both have a vested interest in making sure your friend, the television star, isn't wrongfully convicted." He pushed his chair back, allowing his toned body to recline its back. "In fact, your lovely sister," he nodded at Tina, "was just here trying to convince me that she was at the scene of the crime and could identify a witness."

"I didn't go that far," Tina interrupted, taking the bait he obviously set to get her to talk.

"You're correct. I must have been mistaken with someone else who provided that information on the case." He looked directly at Tina and she sneered back. The chemistry between the two was confusing. But then again, Tina's impact on men of all ages and races was always unpredictable.

"We have come by some material that may be important to the case. It's this piece of clothing." Ignoring their exchange, I handed over the large plastic zip lock bag in which Tina had placed the t-shirt; Don's hair was still held carefully in its folds.

"What leads you to believe this is important?" Detective Food Network Guy accepted the package.

"For one, after it came into our possession, we were followed and apprehended." His eye bugged out on the word apprehended.

"Really?" He questioned and repeated, "Really now." He glanced at Tina who had once again taken her school girl pose.

"Yes." I stated emphatically. "We were commanded to stay out of this case and if we did not, there would be trouble. Tina was physically attacked in the process." We had proof of Tina's bruised thigh that could not have been self-inflicted if he needed proof. Well, it didn't point to who actually did it, but it would certainly corroborate our story. Surely we were motivated to help Jess, but there was no reason for us to lie; although I forgot Tina had already lied to him, but that shouldn't count.

Detective Food Network Guy tossed the bag onto the side of his desk, our critical piece of evidence now among printed emails, notebooks, newspapers, several dirty napkins, and crumbled McDonald's bags. "Well, I certainly appreciate that you have provided us with this, uh ... evidence, as you call it, but I think it best that you let us do our work here."

"We are eager to support." I wasn't going to have him dismiss us so soon without some probing. I attempted to answer his unasked questions. "But if you would run a DNA test or some kind of identifying test on the hair on the shirt it might be an important clue." I looked at Tina for support, now wishing I had not asked her to be low-key. Surely she would be able to make the connection for this to be a critical piece of information. But even she was looking at me as if I ate babies for breakfast.

"The shirt belongs to one of my former patients. I am a psychologist so it would not be ethical, at least at this point, to reveal his name. I am willing to do so, privately and confidentially, of course, once you confirm that there is a biological connection between the hair samples, which we believe to be those of Don Davenport, and the owner of the shirt.

Maybe the owner's prints can be located elsewhere in connection with Don's death."

I took a deep breath, priding myself that my presentation of the facts did not compromise Trenton's confidentiality. After all, Trenton also believed that there might be some kind of connection with his parents and his Uncle Don's death. If there was a connection to be made between Rachel's gambling habit and Don's death, then it needed to be made by the police. Rachel never once hinted at a love for gambling. I never interpreted her shopping as a symptom of addiction, but rather a symptom of boredom. I could have probed more. I had come to be quite fond of Rachel in a weird sort of way, but now getting Jessica erased as a suspect was a priority.

"And how did the shirt actually come into your possession?" Detective Food Network Guy leaned back in his chair with a curious grin.

"I happen to be a member of the same athletic club where Kathy's patient belongs ... not that I know the identity of that patient ... but Kathy does. So I was able to obtain it ... with permission of course." I sighed. We hadn't rehearsed this part, although we had anticipated that they might want to know how it was obtained.

"Really now?" Detective Food Network Guy came forward in his chair releasing the incline and scaring the bejeebees out of me.

"Okay, I got it out of his locker and you can't use the shirt in a court of law, we know that, but you can at least start to go down another path with suspects other than Jessica Davis." Tina folded her arms defiantly. "Always blaming things on the black woman ... or maybe it's the black man, but in this case, it's the same—black gets blamed. Jessica didn't do anything. You're barking up the wrong tree. Digging in the wrong place. Singing the wrong song. Got the accent on the wrong syllable ..." Tina was full of idiomatic expressions.

"Okay, okay. I get your point. And actually being a black woman works in her favor..." The words poured out of his mouth as if he forgot we were in the room. He abruptly stopped and stood up, stretching every bit of his six-foot-two frame.

"Again, ladies, please let us take care of the investigation." He gestured toward the door requesting that we leave. We sat dumbfounded. I couldn't believe we were being dismissed so quickly, and, even more importantly, our evidence was being dismissed.

"If you don't mind, I have an important scheduled appointment that I must keep." He ushered us through the door. Like school kids, we were being dismissed back to our classrooms with reassurance that the adults were in charge of the world.

Frustrated, I let out a sigh and followed Tina through the door, bumping into her back as she stopped short in her tracks. Tina was a few inches taller than me, and even with the added two-inch heels, I could see the face of Big Hand staring directly at us. I released a silent scream and quickly turned around seeking refuge with Detective Food Network Guy. Tina stood frozen, inches away from Big Hand.

"By the way, ladies, you're preaching to the choir." Detective Food Network Guy said and smiled and said as he called out to Big Hand. "Come on in, Captain. Sorry to keep you waiting."

CHAPTER 25B

I wasn't at all thrilled about coming back to see Detective Food Network Guy, but Kathy was gung ho on this plan of taking the shirt to the police. Unknowingly she gave me an out with her parental guidance instruction to sit quietly. Great! Easier to stare Food Network Guy down so he didn't reference our last conversation. It wasn't looking too good for Jess, and my offering a simple favor didn't help her case. In fact, it was damn embarrassing. I usually don't get my chemistry vibes wrong, and he was definitely messing with me. As we entered his office, I made a bee-line for the worn-out leather office chair and sat my butt down. I could tell I was throwing Kathy off by sitting here like I used to in church when Daddy would stare down the pew commanding me to be quiet.

"Detective, thanks for seeing us. I'm Kathy Carpenter Hoffman and this is my sister, Tina." Detective Food Network Guy gave a coy smile that made me want to slap him so I stared at my ankle boots. "We're here with some information on the

Don Davenport murder." Okay, I admit that was my similar approach the last time I was here. I wasn't completely stupid and knew that he wouldn't believe my full story, but Kathy seems convinced that he will be just jump up and down with joy that she is here with the answer to what came first, the chicken or the egg, along with who killed Don Davenport.

"Oh, yes. I understand you both have vested interest in making sure your friend, the television star, isn't wrongfully convicted." He pushed his chair allowing his work-out body to recline its back. "In fact, your lovely sister was just here trying to convince me that she was at the scene of the crime and could identify a witness."

"I didn't go that far," I impulsively responded, kicking myself for opening my mouth. Okay, so I kinda let him know that I might have seen someone that was in the condo although I really wasn't there. I didn't say I could identify anyone. But Jess was there and she did see someone, although she had yet to tell the police. She was scared silly believing that it would only incriminate her more.

"You're correct. I must have been mistaken with someone else who provided that information on the case." He looked directly at me, knowing that both Jess and the unknown to us woman figure were certainly captured on some video camera. When Kathy glanced at me, he winked. See there! He was messing with me again.

"We have come by some material that may be important to the case. It's this piece of clothing." Kathy handed over the large plastic zip lock bag with the t-shirt and Don's hair hopefully still there in its folds.

"What leads you to believe this is important?" Detective Food Network Guy accepted the package.

"For one, after it came into our possession, we were followed and apprehended." His eye bugged out with Kathy's choice of words. She could be a real drama queen when she put her mind to it.

"Really?" He questioned and repeated, "Really now." He glanced at me as if I wasn't telling the truth, but it was Sister Nun who was speaking, and she and George Washington were probably the only people in history who have never told a lie.

"Yes." Kathy stated emphatically. "We were commanded to stay out of this case, and if we did not, there would be trouble. Tina was physically attacked in the process." I could show him my bruise to prove it, but he would probably think it was self-inflicted as a way to come-on to him again by showing him my legs. I can't help it if I spray my Chanel perfume on my boobs instead of my wrists. I was just trying to show him that the newspaper poem smelled like me. If he knew Jess, he would have known that she smells like Dove soap. I was just making a point, and he took it as a come-on. If I were going to flirt with him, it wouldn't have been that obvious. I am, after all, no amateur at flirting.

Detective Food Network Guy tossed the bag onto the side of his desk, our critical piece of evidence now among printed emails, notebooks, newspapers, several dirty napkins, and crumbled McDonald's bags. "Well, I certainly appreciate that you have provided us with this, uh ... evidence, as you call it, but I think it best that you let us do our work here."

"We are eager to support." Kathy wasn't going to have this dismissed so soon without some probing. "But if you would run a DNA test or some kind of identifying test on the hair on the shirt it might be an important clue." A smug look appeared on Detective Food Network Guy's face. It was as if we were interviewing for a position where the candidate had already been chosen and had already started the job, but Kathy was working hard to convince him otherwise.

"The shirt belongs to one of my former patients. I am a psychologist so it would not be ethical, at least at this point, to reveal his name. I am willing to do so, privately and confidentially, of course, once you confirm that there is a biological connection between the hair samples, which we believe to be those of Don Davenport and the owner of the shirt. Maybe the owner's prints can be located elsewhere in connection with Don's death." Kathy's sigh was audible. She was working hard to provide them with another suspect, any suspect besides Jessica.

"And how did the shirt actually come into your possession?" Detective Food Network Guy leaned back in his chair with a curious grin.

"I happen to be a member of the same athletic club where Kathy's patient belongs ... not that I know the identity of that patient…but Kathy does. So I was able to obtain it… with permission of course." It was my turn to sigh. We hadn't rehearsed this part, although we had anticipated that they might want to know how it was obtained. This was the best I could do with only two seconds to respond.

"Really now?" Detective Food Network Guy came forward in his chair releasing the incline, signaling I better come clean.

"Okay, I got it out of his locker, and you can't use the shirt in a court of law, we know that, but you can at least start down another path with suspects other than Jessica Davis." There, I said it. He could fake arrest me again just to make me stop being so defiant. "Always blaming things on the black woman…or maybe it's the black man, but in this case, it's the same—black gets blamed." This was going nowhere. "Jessica didn't do anything. You're barking up the wrong tree. Digging in the wrong place. Singing the wrong song. Got the accent on the wrong syllable…"

"Okay, okay. I get your point. And actually being a black woman works in her favor…" The words poured out of his mouth as if he forgot we were in the room. He abruptly stopped and stood up, stretching every bit of his six-foot-two frame.

"Again, you ladies let us take care of the investigation." As he gestured for us to leave, we sat dumbfounded. Detective Food Network Guy obviously had the upper hand here, and we were not value added to this case at all.

"If you don't mind, I have an important scheduled appointment that I must keep." He ushered us through the door, but I was already moving, anticipating that he was going to ask us to leave. I didn't want to give him the satisfaction of throwing us out. Kathy reluctantly followed. I moved quickly so that his last comments would trail to my back. I confidently walked out the door with the gait that said revenge would be ours, only to be stopped dead in my tracks inches away from Big Hand.

"By the way, ladies, you're preaching to the choir." Detective Food Network Guy smiled and said as he called out to Big Hand. "Come on in, Captain. Sorry to keep you waiting."

CHAPTER 26

The shuttle from ticketing to Concourse B in Atlanta's Hartsfield-Jackson Airport was especially and surprisingly crowded for a Sunday evening. I grabbed the leather strap anchored to the ceiling of the train to steady my stance. As it picked up speed, I positioned myself not to land on the shoulder of the Einstein-look-alike guy next to me. Misery loves company and the depression that sat heavy on my chest wanted so badly to be in the company of Jessica and Tina, but that would not be the case. At her attorney's request, Jessica's hearing would be delayed by at least a week. There was little to do to move Jess's release forward and a lot to do emotionally if we were going to continue to get through the days. Sulk, commiserate, weep, blame, worry, wonder, anticipate, and plead. As I headed back to Cleveland, my emotions pushed me to be joined with Jess and Tina, even if it would have to be via email, phone, or text messaging. Unfortunately my emotional state needed to take a back seat to patients with their own emotional work that I needed to support.

The gate wall board changed to indicate that Delta Flight 287 was delayed by forty minutes just as the gate agent announced that the plane intended to fly back to Cleveland was still airborne. Grateful for the extra time, I took a seat with a convenient end table on which I placed my purse that held a now ringing cell phone.

"Hey, Tina," I quickly answered. "I just got to the gate. The plane's delayed so I've not only made it in time but have time to—"

"Great. Go get today's *AJC*." Tina interrupted.

"What?"

"The newspaper. Go pick up the newspaper and when you get it call me back. I want to check out something."

"What's that?" I asked, dragging my luggage while strapping my purse over my shoulder. I knew better than to spend time weighing the value of the directives being given to me by Tina. It was easier just to do it.

"Wait until you get it. The picture will explain itself."

I picked up the bundle of the newspaper and debated removing and throwing away all the advertisements and supplements, but knowing Tina, she might have just wanted to show me a furniture advertisement with an unbelievable price that she intended to sue someone for because they overcharged her for the same purchase last week. I lugged the entire *Atlanta Journal Constitution* back with the *More Magazine*, bag of trail mix, and bottled water that I purchased. Luckily the same seat was available, as I especially needed the end table now for all of my goods. The gate agent had left her post, which was never a good sign. Most likely we were in for a much longer wait than announced. Settling in for the anticipated lengthy wait, I picked up the call from Tina on the first ring.

"I was just getting ready to call."

"What took you so long? Did you get the paper?"

"I picked up something to eat, and yes, I picked up the paper."

"Go to entertainment section E2 under events. The woman in that J. Mendel fuchsia dress with that metrosexual guy that looks familiar..."

I was dumbstruck. It was a picture of the Nelsons from the hospital fundraiser in Cleveland. In a brief side article, Rachel was named as the chair of the upcoming Children's Healthcare Hospital Benefit in Atlanta.

"That woman is the one who was with Don. I'm positive. She's also the one who showed up at his funeral."

Okay—not news for me that Rachel was with Don and not surprising that she would have been the one Tina saw and believed her to be cheating on Jessica. I didn't respond. Tina was clever and quick. I knew my sister well. It was a half second before her light bulb went on.

"She's at some shindig in Cleveland. Do you know her? Wait, she looks familiar." If Tina were physically present, she would be punching me in the arm. I could almost feel the punches through the phone. "She favors that Sr. Joy. She must be her sister." She paused. "And you're not saying anything, so you must know her professionally." She eased out the word *professionally,* emphasizing its significance and interpretation of my silence.

"Holy Moses! That guy is the one from Fr. R's party. I knew he looked familiar. And the guy who is their son was with the woman at the funeral." Silence. "I know I'm right 'cause you ain't saying nothing. I was just going to ask you if you knew her because it says Rachel Nelson, pictured here with her husband, Jamal, and son, Trenton, at a noted Cleveland benefit, will chair… blah, blah, blah."

"So what do you know? And don't hide behind the patient-attorney privilege or whatever it is. Jess's life is at stake. Do you know anything?"

"I wish I did. I wish there was something." Any connection I had, besides being confidential, was also circumstantial and obviously leading to nothing. We had provided the shirt and any motivation for the Nelsons to be involved to the police and it fell flat.

"There must be something." Although her words were meant to be hopeful, the tone was just the opposite.

The gate agent returned, and picking up the microphone, announced that the plane had arrived, and it would be just a few minutes before we could start boarding.

"I wish there was something, Tina. I just don't think there is much there with the Nelsons." I didn't exactly believe what I just said, but I did not want to lead Tina down a wrong path and certainly did not want her to share any possibility of another possible suspect with Jessica.

"Listen, I've got to go. We're boarding. I'll be sure to re-think everything and let you know if I get a lead."

"Did that shirt belong to the gay son or the metrosexual Dad?"

"Doesn't matter, Tina. There's no connection and it didn't get us anywhere but embarrassed with the police. Don't worry. I am just as much committed to getting her released at any cost. Even despite being scared silly that we can't even trust the police right now."

Overhearing our conversation, the earthy-looking mother in front of me turned and gave me a parenting look while she shuffled her two young sons in front of her. If I didn't end the conversation soon, she might report me as a potential terrorist or better yet, maybe she was working for Big Hand.

"Gotta go, Tina. Call you when I land." I powered down the phone and gave a facial grimace as a reply to the mother still staring at me. As we moved forward in line, she turned and spoke.

"Aren't you Dr. Carpenter?"

I nodded fearfully, hoping that she was just going to give me a lecture about phone etiquette or some bad example I had unknowingly modeled for her children.

"I've seen you on the morning shows. My husband is the world's kindest man, but he also had a bad internet gambling habit." Determined to have this conversation with me, she pushed the boys to keep walking in front of her down the ramp to the airplane. They happily skipped off with their new-found freedom of being off the parent leash for even a few minutes. "You really helped me to wake up and notice that behind all the sweetness and politeness was a reckless side that almost cost us our family."

"Ah, I'm not so sure how I could have done that, but thank you. I know it had to be your work, so really thank yourself."

"No, when you told that one caller to pay attention to her husband's schedule to see if he had a problem with gambling, and that a gambler's schedule becomes the family's schedule, you were right. And that caller was me. When I started to notice how his schedule revolved around gambling, I confronted him and found out we were in tremendous debt and he was at risk of losing his job. He got some help. We all got help. Checking his schedule was the key. So, thank you."

"No, thank you. Thank you for sharing that with me. I am so glad for you and your family." She beamed.

"And for me," I whispered to myself.

Suddenly I was eager to get back to see Randy. I was certain a clue would be waiting for me there.

CHAPTER 27

It was unlike Randy to be late for Mass. In our decades of friendship, I had never known him to oversleep or not to be so timely that you could set a clock by his punctuality. The small congregation of ten or so regular daily communicants sat with closed eyes, either quietly meditating or perhaps just catching a few extra winks.

I was too anxious to do either. I had rehearsed over and over again the conversation I intended to have with Randy knowing that the concept of straight talk must have been created by him. In order to get any information from him about Jamal without directly asking would be difficult. The problem was that I did not have a lot of context for what I needed to know. Well, except for the young mom who triggered the thought that examining a gambler's schedule might shed some light on the situation and lead to new discoveries?

Surely, Jamal was privy to Don's schedule, since Don had worked for Ubold for the past five years as his vice president of merchandising; a job provided more as the result of their personal relationship than to Don's competencies. Even Joy admitted to me that, outside of Rachel's claims as a potential father to Trenton, she did not really know Don. She wasn't even aware that Don was on the payroll at her father's company until shortly before his death.

Randy arrived, entering the vestibule and simultaneously pulling his vestment over his head. With his brow squirreled and facial muscles tightened, he attempted to demonstrate a controlled presence. He quickly whispered an audible sorry before he made the sign of the cross and began the liturgy. Uncharacteristically, he rambled through a ninety-second homily and methodically completed the ritual without the prayerful reflection he regularly infused into what would otherwise be a script.

My well-rehearsed conversation was for naught, or so I thought. Randy nodded to me to join him in the sacristy while he disrobed. Whatever he needed to talk about was urgent.

"Kathy, if one of your patients tells you she is about to cause harm to someone else or has caused harm, you are obligated to tell authorities, right?"

"Uh, yeah."

"Okay, that's what I thought. That is what I said."

Mr. Straight Talk was communicating in circles, and I was dumbfounded into silence.

"It's Jamal. He called early this morning. He's now convinced that Rachel may have been responsible for Don's death."

"Oh, sweet Jesus," I exclaimed as my legs buckled, and gratefully my butt landed on the wooden stool placed in the corner. Was Jamal trying to pin something he did on his wife?

"Kath, I think we can agree this can be a confessional, therapy kind of conversation. If Rachel has committed a crime and her husband knows about it, then we need to get her to confess or tell the authorities."

"Uh…Rachel evidenced a few personality flaws but nothing that would lead me to believe she was capable of murder." Stuttering my way through an explanation for this accusation, I quickly catalogued sessions where I might have missed that this could be an even remote possibility. "What makes him think that she would do this?"

Randy pulled on a Cleveland Cavaliers jacket over his polo shirt and gestured for me to follow him over to the rectory to continue the conversation. I glanced at my watch noting the time and realized there was a patient expected in just a half hour.

"Let me call Connie and have her reschedule my eight-thirty. With a little luck she might even be able to catch her before she leaves the house."

We had more than a little luck as the patient had asked if she could come in the afternoon, and there was an available slot. Now if only more luck could follow and clear up this mess. My stomach was turning with little hope of being relieved by the cup of tea Randy handed me as we sat in the kitchen to continue the conversation.

"It's pretty deep. An internal company investigation is now complete. It turns out Don had been embezzling millions over a four-year period, but he wasn't alone; it was more of a scheme that included a lot of folks in the business but also others. Here's the worst part. He believes there's evidence that Rachel might have been involved and I'm sorry to say, Jessica."

"Jessica wrote checks to the company as a payback for loans to Don. She had no idea that it was anything more than Don borrowing from the company and she was helping him to pay it back. She started to realize his gambling was beyond an emotional thrill and ..." I quickly defended Jessica, "she didn't think his gambling was compulsive and certainly didn't have any idea about embezzlement. Oh, God, this is awful." The tears hit my cheeks as I ran my hands across my face, leaving Bobbie Brown foundation makeup all over my hands. Randy sat watching me wipe the makeup off with a paper napkin.

"I don't have all the details. In fact, this is the first I am hearing about Jessica's checks. That didn't seem to be a concern for Jamal. He just mentioned Jessica almost in passing. He was more freaked out that his wife might be implicated in Don's murder. And with good cause."

"How is that?"

"She admitted that she was there the night he was murdered, but only to talk to him about leaving for Cleveland to get her life back together. The police are not interested in her. They have the surveillance camera, but somehow Jamal is convinced that Rachel knows more than she is admitting or is just naïve enough not to put two and two together. She may have been used in some way in this scheme."

I gasped. She was the witness. The white woman who saw Jessica. The witness the police had that placed Jess at Don's house that night.

"That makes two of them being used, Randy. Jessica could have never done this. And Rachel doesn't know what she knows if she knows it, if that makes any sense."

"Sadly, it does, Kathy."

CHAPTER 28A

"I've got just about twenty minutes before Claudia Swayne is due, right?" I asked Connie, quickly moving past the front office as I entered. For some reason the angst had lifted and was replaced with an energy that was propelling me into action.

"Yep. And she already called to say she would be about five minutes late because she got called into a meeting with her boss at the last minute, but she knows it will still be over in time for her to keep this appointment because he has to leave to catch a plane."

"Great." My luck was really multiplying today. I winked at Connie while dialing Tina's number as I walked back to my office.

"Hey, sister. First, how's Jess?" Tina had made bail, and Jessica had been released to Tina's care yesterday.

"She's hanging in there. Prayerful. Reflective. I'm the one who's freaking out. You know how these things can just keep getting worse and worse. This woman I know because we go to the same stylist works at Food Source and called and told me that there was a big, hush-hush investigation, and they think it goes back to Don. Vendor contracts are being cancelled left and right. Apparently he had some kind of kickback scheme where you got your cake mix or peanut butter or whatever stuff you wanted in the grocery store on better shelves or even just stocked at Publix instead of Wayfield Foods. Supposed to be millions involved. No wonder they are all over Jess about those checks. They think she was in on it."

"So, I guess it isn't as hush-hush as Jamal would like it to be." I said aloud.

"Jamal. What's he got to do with this?"

"He's the CEO of Ubold. You didn't know that? Then again, how would you? Ubold Holdings is a huge company with over sixty thousand employees and about fifteen or more divisions. Don worked in the Food Source division with all the grocery stores," I continued to talk.

I had Googled all of this when I first hooked back up with Joy and started seeing Rachel. Jon further explained the organizational structure to me. It took a while before Randy and I became aware that Don actually worked for Ubold. It made sense that when Jess wrote the checks to Ubold it would not have occurred to her that it was actually Don's place of employment and not a vendor.

"Holy Moley. I didn't know that. Okay, okay. Wait. Vegas lights going on. That means that Jamie, Don's fake friend, really exists, and his name is Jamal, and the white lady Rachel was the one messing around with Don, and she's his boss's wife. That's some crazy shit. Wait. You knew this all along. How come you didn't make this obvious…oh, double shit, one of them must be one of your nut-cases! I knew it. Which one belongs to the hairy t-shirt? Must be that stinking Rachel. Hey, does that Sr. Joy know any of this? This is beyond prayer."

"It's a mess, Tina. But somewhere in this mess is some hope for clearing Jess. Listen, what I wanted you to do is to probe Jess a bit more. It's good you already know about the embezzlement, even more than I just found out." I slipped a bit, not intending to break the code of silence between Randy and me so quickly.

I continued, hoping Tina wouldn't want to know my source. "Find out how much she can remember about Don's schedule, who he met with, where he went." My attempt to ask Randy about getting this information from Jamal took a U-turn when he dropped the Rachel may be responsible scenario on me. If my instincts were right, and luck continued to be on my side, Jessica might prove to be a much better source. "Also drill her for who she remembers seeing that night. She's probably sitting on some small piece of information that could get her cleared, and she doesn't even realize it."

"I'm all over it and even ahead of you, Sister Nun. I was going to take her as far away as the city limits will allow her to go on bail, just to have lunch and chill out. We both need it. I'll see what she says and connect with you later."

"Sounds like a plan."

It would be ten minutes before Claudia would get here, even being on time. Resting my elbows on my desk and fingers massaging my forehead, I worked to clear all the racing thoughts. Doing so even for thirty seconds would reduce the stress. Thoughts like rain graciously sprinkled from my mind leaving a vacancy and replacing it with a sense of peace that I had not experienced since Jessica was first implicated.

Relishing the moment, I pushed back on my office chair and opened my eyes surveying the ceiling, the room, and then my desk. There it was. Trenton's letter that I had hastily thrown on top of the files just five days ago was now neatly placed on top of mail.

Trenton's maturity, politeness, and even-tempered spirit would be reflected in a longer thank you than his mother's brief message. It would be so like him to write a letter to bring closure to his therapy sessions. The blade of the letter opener sliced through the envelope revealing two pages of type:

Dear Dr. Carpenter,

I regret that our sessions had to end so abruptly, but Mom is insistent that we return to Atlanta as there is pressing business that she finds it necessary to support Dad in managing. Since my mom has never expressed such a need and Dad has never, ever included Mom in any business matters, I suspect that it must be really important. They can only tell me that it is a family matter, and ironically whatever this crisis is, for the first time in my existence, I really feel like we are acting like a family. Mom and Dad are actually talking a lot, and sometimes it leads to tears, but they are crying together.

I always knew that Mom just wanted to get Dad's attention by all of her shopping and spending time with Uncle Don to get Dad jealous. I know that feeling. For a long time, Mom just thought that my claiming to be gay was just to get Dad's attention. I actually thought that for a while as well, but it didn't last long. Dad was always more concerned about my education and getting a good job than he was about whom I loved. It was like he knew that I was gay even before I did and had a longer time to get used to the fact and was just waiting around for me to tell him. That didn't stop the fact that I wanted and needed his attention. Somehow, since Uncle Don's death, it seems like getting that is a possibility. Now I just have to figure out how to get to know him and how he will get to know me. I mean, how I can share with him the me that I hope he will be proud of and want to get to know better.

I really want to thank you for all you did for our family. Auntie Joyce says you were an answer to a prayer that she never dared to pray. When Grandpa died, she was more upset about getting the money released under the conditions that Grandpa set than she was about his death. By the way, I know you were supposed to cure me of being gay and I was glad that you never even mentioned it. You can just say you tried and it didn't work. Or you can just tell the truth which is somehow what I think you will do. And that is okay 'cause no amount of money is worth me not being who I am.

I know that I am who God made me to be. Auntie Joyce tells me that. My mom believes in me, and my dad has accepted who I am.

I also know that I am a Nelson. I didn't need a paternity test to tell me, and after I went through all of the trouble of getting one done, I figured out I was doing it just to stop my mom from talking about it. Then I realized that all that "Don is your dad talk" was about her and Dad and had nothing to do with me. She just wanted us to be a family. I sent the unopened results to Uncle Don with a note that said no matter what was in that envelope that my dad was my dad. I sent a copy to Auntie Joyce with a note that said here is our proof, if ever it is needed, to help Mom come to some kind of resolution.

Weeks later, I went to see him and told him that I couldn't hang with him anymore and asked him to stay away from my mom because it was messing everybody up. Mom had even gotten his assistant to try to get him to stop gambling because he was losing so much money and would soon lose his job. The gambling wasn't recreational anymore. She also was getting scared. Her scheme to get Dad's attention was backfiring.

He begged me not to cut him out of his life. He said he

needed me more than ever. That he was really my father and that the paternity test had proven it. And here's the zinger. He wanted me to give him half of my inheritance money and he would never tell my dad or mom about the results. That made me so angry. He had failed the test of our relationship so miserably. He wasn't my father. He knew it and I knew it. At the time, I really wanted to kill him. I didn't do it, but he ended up dying that day.

Auntie Joyce says that sometimes God takes care of things in mysterious ways and that we should leave the mystery alone. I guess that is her interpretation of the saying "let go and let God." You really helped me to leave all this behind and to move on. And move on I will do.

Thanks so much for your help.

Yours Truly,
Trenton Nelson

CHAPTER 28B

"Robin, see what you can do to clear most of the day for me. I'll swing by XL's house later this afternoon if I can break away, but I really have to spend some time with Jess today. Make something up, and let him know that he still is my priority, blah, blah, blah. You're good at that."

Robin had been my faithful assistant for four years now. A record in the world of design. Maybe because she had no aspirations of being a designer herself and was happy, happy, happy to support. At times like these when I had to spring Jessica from jail and keep her sequestered at my house, I greatly appreciated her tactfulness and confidence. Robin was the best.

"Gotta go, Robin. My sister is on the other line. Call me back if you need anything." I swapped calls on the iPhone to hear Kathy's voice.

"Hey, sister. First, how's Jess?"

"She's hanging in there. Prayerful. Reflective. I'm the one who's freaking out. You know how these things can just keep getting worse and worse. This woman I know because we go to the same stylist works at Food Source and called and told me that there was a big, hush-hush investigation, and they think it goes back to Don. Vendor contracts are being cancelled left and right. Apparently he had some kind of kickback scheme where you got your cake mix or peanut butter or whatever stuff you wanted in the grocery store to be on better shelves or even just stocked at Publix instead of Wayfield Foods. Supposed to be millions involved. No wonder they are all over Jess about those checks. They think she was in on it."

"So, I guess it isn't as hush-hush as Jamal would like it to be," Kathy said and left me wondering if I missed the first part of a movie.

"Jamal. What's he got to do with this?"

"He's the CEO of Ubold. You didn't know that? Then again, how would you? Ubold Holdings is a huge company with over sixty thousand employees and about fifteen or more divisions. Don worked in the Food Source division with all the grocery stores," Kathy continued to talk as if we had both seen the same movie. And I hadn't even seen the preview of it.

"Holy Moley. I didn't know that. Okay, Okay. Wait. Vegas lights going on. That means that Jamie, Don's fake friend, really exists, and his name is Jamal, and the white lady Rachel was the one messing around with Don, and she's his boss's wife. That's some crazy shit. Wait. You knew this all along. How come you didn't make this obvious…oh, double shit, one of them must be one of your nut-cases! I knew it. Which one belongs to the hairy t-shirt? Must be that stinking Rachel. Hey, does that Sr. Joy know any of this? This is beyond prayer."

"It's a mess, Tina. But somewhere in this mess is some hope for clearing Jess. Listen, what I wanted is for you to probe Jess a bit more. It's good you already know about the embezzlement, even more than I just found out." Kathy paused, remembering that I wasn't the one who saw this movie with her. She was talking all out of context. "Find out how much she can remember about Don's schedule, who he met with, where he went. Also drill her for who she remembers seeing that night. She's probably sitting on some small piece of information that could get her cleared and she doesn't even realize it." When Kathy is in one of these take no prisoner's moods, you just had to go with the flow.

"I'm all over it and even ahead of you, Sister Nun. I was going to take her as far away as the city limits will allow her to go on bail, just to have lunch and chill out. We both need it. I'll see what she says and connect with you later."

"Sounds like a plan." In-Charge Sister Nun hung up abruptly.

"Girl, you are sporting that afro. It actually makes you look ten years younger." Concerned that folks would recognize her, and especially to deter the media, I had given Jessica a retro seventies look. I didn't think that it looked too costumey, but Jess needed a little encouragement. It was a far cry from her anchorwoman look.

"You sure it doesn't attract attention in the other way? I thought the goal was to not stand out."

"It's not blonde. Not that that would be a stand-out. I actually wear that curly 'fro sometimes. It looks good."

"Like I said, it stands out." Jess actually managed a smile. "Where are we anyway? At least this place is less likely to be known to anyone who might recognize me. Does WBS even get broadcasted out here?"

"Milton Outlet Mall is not too far from here, where you get all the designer deals. That's how I know this place. It's the only decent restaurant other than the chains and fast food within five miles. Feel like a little shopping after we eat?"

"I may not have any need for a new wardrobe, at least a designer one. I am looking at my outfits getting provided for me, remember?" Despondent, Jess picked at the bread I placed on her plate demanding that she eat a full meal.

"That ain't happening. Not on my watch. Listen, drink a little of that wine, 'cause I'm hoping to interrogate you a bit." She frowned and shook her head.

"Don't get all traumatized on me. I mean that in a good way. Kath and I are on to something, and we think we can really get the heat off you."

"Didn't we already go this route? And if you don't recall how it turned out, know that I am now a bonded woman."

"This time the squeeze is worth the juice. Trust me." The

afro curls tossed back and forth as Jess shook her head, more in a frustrated manner than a defiant one. It was the best I would get, so I started drilling.

"Okay, I need you to recreate the scene that night from the moment you parked your car. Think about everything—the weather, the building, who was walking around."

"You and Kathy watch too much *Law & Order*. I've already gone over all of this with the police," she leaned forward, "and with you. There's nothing more that stands out. It's like I said before. I drove up and first just stayed parked on the street for a minute or so. Just kinda thinking and reminiscing, then I saw a car entering the gate and impulsively followed. I knew that bar or whatever you call it, you know, the arm, would not go down for a few seconds so I just drove myself to the other side. Got out the car, went down the hallway, and could already hear voices or just sounds coming from his apartment, so chickened out 'cause I didn't even have a reason to be there... except for maybe 'Hi, I was thinking about you, no, really about us.' It was so stupid. I left. Got back in my car and after I pulled out, heard some noise and looked up and saw him fall." The twisted napkin in her hands served to gather the tears that were now her customary demeanor.

"I'm sorry Jess, but I need to ask. Did you see who got out of the car? Was it a white woman? A good-looking college kid? Or a black man?" Three distinct choices, surely she would nail one of them.

"No, it was a white guy. A tall, husky white man and he didn't go into the same building."

Maybe they were the ones already with Don. "You sure? How about in the hallway? See a white woman or the college dude or black man there? Or maybe after, did you see anybody leaving the gate after…" Distracted by our waitress who blew right by us over to a table in the corner, I was just getting ready to go off about her ignoring us when I saw that she was just finishing up with a white woman and a black woman who, from the way they were dressed, looked like they were frequent visitors to the designer outlet mall.

"Oh, My God…Jess, listen. Don't turn around. Make like a statue and just listen. I'm going to the restroom. Finish your wine, but when the waitress comes back, tell her there's a family emergency and we have to leave. Get the check and pay. If I'm not out by that time, I'll meet you in the car." I needed a pen. My purse had to have a pen.

"Pen, pen, quick!" I said to Jess who had already gone into statue mode. She stared at me like I had lost my mind but adjusted and quickly started looking for a pen in her purse. With little time, my black eye liner served to write Out Of Order on the unused napkin from the set table. "I'm good," I said as she resumed statue mode.

"Thank you, Jesus!" I cried, pulling out the blue painter's tape I had thrown in my purse to remind myself to pick up more for Modell and Ronny who were working on XL's house. I attached a small piece to the napkin sign and took off.

"Tina, what is going on?" Jessica's eyes were as big as saucers.

"Don't move. Pay, leave, and wait in the car. Trust me." I commanded and sped from my seat to the ladies' room. I couldn't tell if the sounds I heard behind me were Jess's cries or laughter.

There were only three stalls in the restroom, which made it much easier. Moving swiftly, I pinned the Out Of Order sign on the last door, entered, and locked myself in. The last time I had pulled this trick, I was almost thirty years younger and trying to catch the chick that was after my man at the time. Luckily I could still position myself athletically on the toilet stool, squatting and bracing my hands on either side, ready and waiting to hear the conversation that I hoped would be pursued by the women who were bound to enter if their grooming habits matched their impeccable dress. Kathy wasn't the only one who never forgot a face, and this time I was sure the white woman was Rachel and the black girl was the one who was there with her at the funeral.

Damn. Why is it when you are near a toilet you suddenly have to go? I hoped to have time to get in a quick twinkle and resume my position, but it wasn't going to happen. Just as I started to pull down my leggings, giddy laughter filled the bathroom. I sprinted back up on the toilet seat, balancing myself with my arms against the stall walls.

"I told you that we would be able to find something like that bad animal print mini and jacket that Jennifer Lopez wore on Jimmy Fallon. It helped that I tore out that picture of her in *People Magazine*; the sales lady in Bebe recognized it right away. I should have been an image consultant. You know, maybe it isn't too late. I know this woman in Chicago who owns this place called Fine Threads and she teaches people to be an image consultant just like she is." It had to be Rachel's voice as she talked to her companion who had just entered the stall next to me.

"I am over the moon excited and have the sharp sky-high boots to go with it. We are going to turn some heads." Flushing toilets and swinging doors signaled they would move to the sink.

"I know you will. Who you going with? That fine specimen Craig who can only take his eyes off your boobs to look at your butt?" Rachel giggled.

"I was hoping that it was with you." I know that the door was blocking my view, but the tone of that request sounded like a come-on if I ever heard one.

Rachel giggled more. "You're crazy. Myech, I meant it when I said, no more clubs and partying. It's all family now, and besides, you know that Jamal is not into clubs like that, even if we did want to join you and Craig."

"You're kidding me, right?" Whoa, girlfriend sounded

pissed. "You're really serious? After all we've been through together, now you're just going to go back to the *Cosby Show* life?"

"Ah, Myech. I'm so sorry. You're a good girlfriend and all…and Lord knows I don't have any good shopping buddies like you, but things are different now. And it was never like that for me, honey. I might have done a little experimenting, you know, like Samantha on *Sex and the City*. It was fun but…"

I could hear the slap and could almost feel the hand on my skin, it hit that hard. Warm urine descended down my right leg, completely soaking the blue paisley-patterned spandex leggings. Pushing hard to lean my torso on the wall so as not to slip in my own urine, I prayed I wouldn't fall against the door.

"You prick! You honestly thought you could just use me to get your Wall Street husband to show you he cared."

"Myechia, that was your fantasy. I do feel badly that I tried to use Don, but that was playful and Jamal knew that." I held my breath during a long pause. "Now, I may have deserved that slap but not the name-calling. I honestly didn't mean to lead you on. We both had too much to drink that night. I am so sorry that you are so hurt and so mistaken because it was never like that, nor could it ever be…" Her voice was trailing, and my legs were shivering from either fright or cold urine.

"I turned in Don for you." Myechia's little girl voice was barely audible.

"Oh, honey. Don't blame yourself for that. My father was on to Don from the start. He was just a small fish in a big, big, pond. I told you not to worry. Daddy's folks were really watching out for him and for you, too." My shitty foot caused me to slip, and there was nowhere else to land it except in the toilet—my six hundred dollar Mui Mui pointed-toe ballet flats that I was so happy to get on sale were probably ruined.

"I loved Don, I really did," Rachel's deep sigh was audible. "But he couldn't help what he brought on himself. We all tried to help him. Time just wasn't on his side. Sometimes our life choices catch up with us. That's what Dr. K. told me."

So it was Rachel who was Sister Nun's nut-case. Sounds like this Myechia woman should be the next one Sister Nun needed to see. My left arm and leg were braced against the wall in an attempt to prevent a full butt slide into the toilet. Thank God their complete self-absorption prevented them from any curiosity about any weird noises that might be heard coming from the stall. And thank God they moved toward the door, just as my butt hit the floor, wedged between the toilet and the stall wall, and my ballet flats still resting in the toilet.

"Baby, you'll be okay. Life goes on and…"

"Don't call me Baby. I'm not your Baby, remember…" They left in the same manner that they entered. Giggling.

CHAPTER 29

"It has taken forever for this day to end." I said to Connie, finally wrapping up back to back patients since the respite this morning that left me reeling from Trenton's thank you letter. It was a gift in an odd way that possibly confirmed the Nelsons were somehow responsible for the death of Don Davenport. Or maybe it could have simply been a demise brought on by his own choices? Right now, I just needed to get home, get a glass of wine, and process what I could with Randy and Tina, without jeopardizing Jessica's case.

"You're telling me. I had hoped the slow start would be indicative of a routine day, but then all hell broke loose at about ten o'clock with three walk-ins. Hey, before we close, you still have to take me home after I drop off my car at the shop."

I had forgotten that I promised to follow Connie to the car dealer and then drop her home. It would only take about a half hour at the most, and surely Connie had done it for me a thousand times. "Sure, I can still give you a ride. No problem; it just slipped my mind given the pace of this day and with everything else that going on, that's all." A momentary side-track caused me to wonder if the course of things for Jess could have changed if I had read Trenton's letter the day of its arrival.

"Yoo-hoo, Kath, you're pretty distracted these days. You want me to call Rob and see if he can meet me there?"

"Sorry. No, you don't need him to leave his office and come all the way across town when we are right here. I'm happy to help out. My mind, as you know, has just been on Jess and I was just processing some new information."

"Pretty deep, huh?" Connie escorted me through the lobby and front door, locking it behind us. "Hey, I am all ears if you need to vent. I'll meet you at the service entrance in five minutes."

Watching Connie sign documents through the glass doors of Case Honda as she dropped off her car was a great reminder that life did indeed go on. It surely seemed to do so for the Nelsons, and I prayed that Jessica would soon continue to experience everyday routine tasks like dropping off your car to be serviced. Thinking about routine tasks reminded me that I was driving around on gas fumes.

"Do you mind if we stop for gas before I drop you home? I'm afraid that we might not even make it to your house, I am so low. That yellow light has been on for two days now."

"You have definitely been preoccupied, Dr. Carpenter,"

Connie said as she buckled her seat belt on the passenger's side. "The girls have choir practice after school and won't be home for another hour. We're good."

It was still unseasonably warm for mid-October which made it a little easier to take the rising gas prices. Maybe this mess would be cleared up by Halloween and Jon and I could even get to Atlanta to celebrate Jessica's clearance. Every waking thought these days led me to thinking about Jess, and my paranoia was now aroused because the man who just came out of the station's convenience store looked exactly like Big Hand. As he briskly walked to the black Chevy, pumping the key ignition, the lights flashed on the car, and I was certain. It was Big Hand.

Instinctively, I stopped pumping the gas and jumped in the car.

"Did you finish? Are you going to close out the transaction?" Connie looked as confused as I was feeling. I jumped out, quickly punched the no button for car wash and for a receipt, returned to the front seat, started the car, and took off in pursuit of the black Chevy.

"Have you lost your mind? Where are we going? Am I being kidnapped?"

"No, I believe I am still oriented to time, person, and place. I do not know where we are going, but we are following that black Chevy that is now about three cars ahead of us. And, if by definition, kidnapping is taking someone away against their will, then I guess you are being kidnapped."

Connie picked up her cell phone and began dialing.

"Who are you calling?" Hopefully she wasn't dialing 911.

"Rob," Connie replied rather calmly for someone being kidnapped.

"Are you planning on suing me? I will get you home, I promise." Connie's husband was a criminal attorney.

"No, I have to let him know to get home for the girls. God only knows how this day will end up, and you are in no position to make promises."

We drove for twenty minutes on a familiar winding road without turning even once. We were headed for Geauga County. If we were both not as tense as we were, it would have been a nice early evening drive with the sun setting and the burst of fall colors embracing the leaves of the many trees that lined the road. We drove in silence and with a bit of excitement about what we would find ahead. I was just about to suggest to Connie that we should call back Rob and call Jon just to let them know our location, when the Chevy turned on Cauldon Road.

"You are kidding me. This cannot be. Connie, I think he is headed for the Motherhouse."

"Whose mother?" Connie was not Catholic, and for many years I had promised to take her out to see the convent which I called home for twelve years.

"He could be going to the Provincial House, you know, the convent where I used to live when I was a nun."

"Now that's something to tell the girls. I got kidnapped and taken to a convent."

My fingers clutched the steering wheel, tightening as we took every twist in the road that led us up the long, steep driveway to the campus of the Annunciation Sisters. I was at once home again in the weirdest of ways. I knew these grounds inside out so I stopped and parked the car in a small lot at the bottom of the hill leading up to a small shrine where visitors often stopped to pray for solace. We were clearly visible to Big Hand, and although I had no idea what might come next, it was best that he didn't see me.

"We've got to change places. You need to drive." Connie looked at me as if I was Thelma and she was Louise, and I was asking her to drive us off a cliff to our deaths.

"Please, I'll finish explaining later. Just know we are saving my friend Jessica from a jail sentence, I think ..."

Connie was already rounding the car. "You owe me big time and I will wait to hear the explanation over alcohol, thank you."

Big Hand's black Chevy was parked right next to the handicapped spot. There were only about ten other cars in the lot that could hold well over twenty-five cars before visitors would need to park on the lower lot by the tennis courts. We chose a spot closer to the lower lot but still in full view of the entrance to the Motherhouse.

"The stained glass windows are where the chapel is, and the rest of this part where we are parked are administrative offices and the laundry. Up on the second floor is the dining room and then all of these windows are the bedrooms."

"Now this is pretty wild. You've got me out here in the middle of Zabuba land giving me a tour like we are on HGTV *House Hunters* and I will need to choose what house I want to buy."

"Oh, my God!" I softly screamed as I slid from the passenger's seat to the floor of my BMW X5.

"What are you doing?"

"Are they there? Look out and tell me. That's Joy and Big Hand, I mean the guy we just trailed here, right?"

"Yep. That's Rachel's sister who first brought her to see you. And yep, that's the mob guy that we just followed out here who could take us out of this world with a mere look. Can we go now?"

"Which way are they headed?" I asked, hoping and praying that Joy would not look our way and recognize the car or Connie.

"Up the hill to the right. Geez, isn't that guy cold? He's just in his shirt sleeves. Just like white people, they see a little sun and act like it's summer no matter what time of year it is."

"Are they far enough up the hill?"

"Yes, they are out of sight now. Can we go now?"

"Yes, let's go," I said, jumping out of the car.

"I meant home. Kathy, where are you going?"

"Come on; I need you to go with me. If they see us I can tell them I was just taking you on a tour."

"Gosh, darn, Kathy. I should be home getting dinner, not running through the fields in pursuit of Maria and the Captain." I led her up the hill toward the east side where there was a small open door cabin that was often used by the nuns when they wanted to come outside to meditate. I suspected it was where Joy and Big Hand were headed. It would make a good place for a clandestine meeting, especially at this time when all of the other nuns were attending Holy Hour before dinner. The faint sounds of the hymn "I Say Yes Lord" in alternating English and Spanish verses trailing over the hills.

"How did you know he was a Captain?"

"Uhmmm ... I didn't. I was making a reference to "Sound of Music"...you know, the nun who goes off to take care of all those Von Trapp kids and ends up marrying the guy Captain Von Trapp."

I laughed at the reference and then stopped abruptly. Joy and Big Hand were a few feet in front of the cabin folded in each other's embrace, lips locked, and tongues in exploratory rounds. Big Hand groped her breasts and made his way down to her pelvic area. Joy's loose hair fell back hitting her shoulder blades, her eyes tightly shut leaving no doubt that she was in pure ecstasy.

"Now this is worth being kidnapped for. And to think I wanted to be home getting dinner ready instead." We both stood staring as Big Hand began to pull off Joy's cardigan, exposing her bra, as she deftly removed the straps, and he began sucking like a hungry baby.

"Come on, let's go." The depths of emotions swallowing me, I didn't know whether the feeling was disappointment, anger, fear, embarrassment, hurt, or all of the above.

"Now you want us to leave? Girl, people pay good money to see this kind of stuff in the movies, and those aren't nuns getting it on." Connie quickly noticed that this was not a laughing matter for me. "I'm sorry," she whispered, "with something so out of the box like this, you've got to find the humor."

"Maybe one day, Connie. Maybe one day, but not today..."

"Kathy, Kathy." Joy's shrills echoed through the air.

"Keep walking," I said to Connie whose emotions had now returned to being freaked out and scared.

"Kathy, please. I can explain."

I took off running, the heels of my shoes sinking in the soft grass. Connie walked behind me, picking up her pace, but refusing to run. Within moments, we were all there together—Joy, the Captain, Connie, and me.

"Kathy, this is Steve Captain, head of security for Ubold and a friend of mine," she paused, trying to read my reaction. "Obviously, a very good friend..." Joy lowered her head in embarrassment.

"And this is Connie Sims, administrator for Psychological Health Care and a friend of mine. A very good friend... but obviously not the same kind of good as your friend." Sarcasm usually erupted when I was angry. At least I had sorted out my feelings. I was pissed.

"Nice to meet you, Steve," Connie extended her hand to Big Hand. "And good to see you again Sister," Connie continued, as if we were exchanging greetings at a conference. Knowing Connie, the pun about it being good to see her was intended. Having worked with me in clinical practice since its inception, Connie would be discreet with this information, but she would take every chance she could get to make some witty reference to this situation.

"Kath, I had planned to talk to you about this," she glanced at Big Hand who appeared, ironically, very docile, "to explain everything. I just had to wait until it could all be finalized."

The vast open space constricted to only the few square feet making up the ground that Joy and I occupied. She had been my closest friend and confidant while I lived here. Other than Fr. Randy, she was the one who held my confidence and who best knew my soul. She was the first person I told when I made the difficult decision to leave the convent. Staring directly into her eyes, I wasn't sure if she was that same person. Had she manipulated me for whatever her purpose was that all of this was serving? Was she that much like the father she despised? Was she as self-absorbed as she believed her sister to be?

"I need to leave now," I said directly to Connie who followed me to the car with Joy and Captain only a few paces behind us.

CHAPTER 30

"You know that I am not that good with technology. Help me to…whoa, I can see you and Jess. How cool is that? How are you doing, Jessica? You look, uh, okay, I guess, given the circumstances." Tina called, using the Face Time app, and it was my first time to use it on my smart phone.

"I'm hanging in there, Kath. Keep thinking I am going to wake up from this nightmare soon."

"Do you want that call projected on your laptop? I can help you." Jon walked into the study. "It will only take a minute."

"Nope, we're good. I don't want to mess with my luck, and I'm not sure how long we'll be anyway."

"Hey White Guy! Thanks for hooking Jess up with your people. They bring a certain degree of credibility to the table when you're trying to keep this emancipation thing going, if you know what I mean." Tina said.

Jon stood physically behind me today as he did emotionally every day of our life together. "No problem. Jess, know we are all praying. This will all end soon. All of the delays are actually in your favor." It had been three weeks since Jessica was released on bail without a mention of a trial date. During this time, Jessica continued to journal, read, and pray. We all joined her in prayer. The team at the news station never lost confidence, and it was the same for thousands of her faithful fans.

Over those same three weeks, I had not spoken to Joy, and being conflicted, I still had not taken any of her calls and left her emails unopened. Time would be our friend.

Tina and I huddled frequently, piecing together information and coming to the conclusion that Don's death must have been what Tina called "accidentally on purpose." We were both convinced that the Nelsons knew more than they owned up to. Most of the time, I felt that Joy's role in all of it was better left unexplained, which is why I stopped all contact. Sometimes it was just better to move on.

Jon was right. The delays for Jessica's trial were a good sign. The very next day, she received a call from her attorney with the good news that she was cleared of all charges. Tina, unsure of the proper etiquette for hosting a party, decided that one was nevertheless in order. It would be a small, intimate gathering of just a few close friends. For Tina that meant about a hundred people.

"This is a case that will go down in history. One of those unsolved mysteries, if you get my drift. In investigative work, that is a euphomym or whatever that word is, for when we know something we can't tell you. Closed files if you will. I knew all along Jessica was innocent. Sweet girl like her gets caught up loving a good man. I know how that is." Tina choked as I looked at her and laughed. "I mean for me it would be caught up loving a good woman of course." Tony Labella was still working hard to convince Tina he was her one and only. She just hadn't realized it yet.

"Well, all of us really appreciated being able to count on you when we needed you, Tony. You were a great help." Tony burst with pride almost popping the buttons on his three-piece vest that was a fashion item about a decade ago.

"Always happy to share my knowledge in the effort to stop crime," Tony declared, heading for the buffet table and the freshly replenished chicken wings.

Jessica, dressed in a bright yellow Jovani dress, radiated with the warmth that was in the room. Only Tina could get away with a "Spring has Sprung" theme for the party in November, a play on Jessica being sprung from jail. Large slinky coils were strategically placed in the conference room of the station, which insisted on hosting the celebration. Everyone was glad that loaning someone money was not a crime even if it was used for purposes unintended. My guess was that the station smelled even higher ratings upon Jessica's return, and there was already talk of a television movie based on Jess's story.

"Have I thanked you for everything?" Jessica gathered Tina and I in a sister hug.

"You have... a million times," Tina and I said almost in unison.

"No, really, thanks for sticking by me, and more importantly thanks for forgiving me. I wasn't always forthright and I know that made it very, very hard for you both to believe in me even when you wanted to. That must have been terribly frustrating, and I'm sorry."

"We understand, Jess. Sometimes we are dealing with emotions we can't explain, and there are times when denial helps us from completely falling apart."

"Come on now. This is a party not a therapy session. Your apology has been received and accepted. It's time to move on to Hollywood and make that movie. Who do you think they should get to play me? I'm thinking about casting Halle Berry."

"Don't flatter yourself, Tina. Jessica's already got dibs on casting Halle in her role." I winked at Jess, so happy to see that the radiant, award-winning anchor smile had returned.

CHAPTER 31

Friday night at Arturo's was always especially crowded, and this Friday before the Thanksgiving holidays was no exception. With the weather in the mid-west still cooperating, residents were particularly jovial, experiencing sun much longer than was typical. I sat across from Jon grateful for so many things, starting with getting this booth despite arriving at the peak hour.

We had ordered and were reviewing our respective weeks when the waitress arrived and placed my order of almond-crusted salmon in front of me and handed Jon his sausage, peppers, and onions in a to-go bag. Before I could ask any questions, Joy slid into the booth. I gave Jon a look that began as confusion and ended with betrayal. He picked up the vibe.

"It was Randy's idea. I'm just the implementer."

It was just like Jon to throw Randy under the bus, and if it had been Jon's idea and Randy was the person to make it happen, Randy would have thrown Jon under the bus.

"I just couldn't leave things like they were. I just needed

you to hear me out. If you choose to never talk to me again after that, I will respect your decision." The pain in Joy's expression made me cringe while experiencing incredible sadness.

"It's okay." I nodded to Jon. "It's taking more energy to avoid you than just getting this over with," I said to Joy in the most emotionless voice I could muster. In friendship, trust can be doled out easily, and just as easily, trust can permanently retreat with one incident.

"I'll leave you two then to enjoy your dinner. Randy and I will be eating at the rectory." He raised the take-outs in the air. "Give me a call when you are finished, and I'll swing by and pick you up." And with a quick kiss on the cheek, Jon disappeared.

I took up my fork and began eating. I wasn't trying to be rude; I just didn't know what else to do. Joy just sat there watching me.

"Are you ordering?" I finally asked.

"I don't know if I can eat anything." That was really something for Joy who not only swore like a truck driver, but ate like one too. She did look as if she had lost a few pounds. Compassion managed to make its way past my mistrust of her.

"Help me to make this easier for you to talk. I love Arturo's, but I don't want to be here all night." I was the one who got ambushed, and Joy was acting as if she were the one surprised by this meeting.

"I've rehearsed this conversation a million times in my mind, and now I don't know where to start."

"Anywhere is okay. Start anywhere." My voice softened as the firm grounding from the many years of our relationship returned.

"Okay. I will start with Steve. Most people call him Captain. I've known him since we first entered the convent. You probably don't remember him, but he actually used to accompany Dad to visiting Sundays. He worked for him forever: First as his driver, then more like a bodyguard, then for the past ten years or more, as head of security for Ubold."

"Your Dad needed a bodyguard?"

"At the time he was building the company, yes. And even in the later years. All of his deals were not on the up and up, Kathy. I think it is what led to Mom's early death. She always lived as if a horse head would end up in their bed one night. Jamal's spent his entire administration cleaning up messes and trying to build an ethical company. Not always easy when the foundation was built on quicksand. I believe that is why Dad always had such admiration for Jamal and insisted that he remain with the company. He made him and his business honest. And, miracles of all miracles, he somehow really loved Rachel and stabilized her in a way that no one else ever could. So you can imagine his upset when Dad found out that she was running around with Don Davenport."

No longer needing food as a distraction, I rested my fork and listened intently.

"When Jamal took over the business, Dad still was pulling strings behind the curtain, in his own way trying to clean up unfinished business and leave this life with a better legacy. That was important to him, and that is where Captain came in. He knew the players and where all the bodies were buried." She paused. "I don't even want to think about the literal translation of that statement. Anyway, all the years of driving, you hear a lot and gain a lot of confidence. He was on Don's trail from when he first got pulled in by one of the shadier vendors but one who had a lot of power. Don was an easy target, likeable and vulnerable with a propensity for gambling. Dad intentionally kept Jamal out of the loop. He was his insurance. Captain managed all of the underground and brought in the police only when necessary. He had enough connections with law enforcement and was respected enough that it was a win/win."

"How about some tea or coffee? You look like you could use something to drink." I projected. This was all a bit overwhelming.

"That's a good idea actually. Thank you."

When the waitress arrived, I was glad that she ordered a small pizza and added a glass of wine along with the tea.

We sat for a few minutes in silence both taking in the immensity of this story while trying to reduce its intensity by savoring our wine.

"Are you in love with him?" I finally asked.

"Yes." She said simply and directly, knowing that I was referring to Steve Captain.

"And you must know how complicated love can be." She continued. I nodded.

"The evening you saw us was our good-bye. We both knew it had to end, especially after Don's death. It would not be wise for us to risk being together. Sometimes people give you, in death, gifts that they could never have given you when they were alive. Dad and Don's deaths were actual gifts to our family.

"We both had the strength to finally cut it off after such a long time. Actually the relationship began shortly after his divorce. His ex was a beautiful, talented artist but also a tortured alcoholic. He was agonizing over the divorce, and I was agonizing over leaving the convent. It wasn't long after you left. You remember the reason why they never wanted us to associate with nuns who had left was because it would and did bring up similar thoughts if you weren't too stable. And I wasn't very stable after you left. I was just becoming aware of Dad's business ventures and realized that much of his charitable giving was stained money. I didn't reach out to you and became disheartened with no one to turn to confidentially, and Steve was a kindred soul."

"Why didn't you just leave?"

"I would like to say it was Dad. He had always made the conditions of his will known. But it wasn't that. Having grown up in wealth, I have never been particularly inspired by money. Believe it or not, I actually came to understand religious life as my vocation. On a very deep level, I knew this to be true. And somehow I also knew, we both really did, that if those barriers were removed, we would not make the best couple. We are both head-strong and fiercely independent. Much of our attraction was based on emotional need at the time, and without the boundaries of religious life preventing us from being man and wife, we might not be so willing to fill each other's emotional need. Our love for each other was not the kind for a good marriage."

The few minutes of silence as she paused to reflect and I to take it all in were no longer strangely uncomfortable but acutely necessary.

"Hey, do you remember that *Law & Order* episode where the father who was this big business owner was being blackmailed by this associate with a bad gambling habit?"

I shook my head indicating that I hadn't; meanwhile, I was trying to recall the episode. Tina and I wore it as a badge of honor that we had seen virtually every episode.

"The father had some ugly business practices that he was afraid of going public with, but nonetheless he refused to pay the guy. Instead he had him followed and watched, and when he got a little too close for comfort, he had some of his crew rough him up a bit just to keep him quiet. Then the dad died, and the guy started trying to blackmail one of the heirs, who happened to be a nun. Funny you don't remember this episode?"

I surely would have remembered this episode. Joy smiled

coyly as I began to appreciate the striking resemblance to the current situation.

"Well, he didn't know the daughter was a nun because you know she wasn't in a habit, and he was old-school thinking that if she was a nun she would dress like one. And this nun was also pretty feisty and just told him to fuck off." I laughed just thinking of the shock value Joy must have got out of that one.

"Anyway, he still kept messing up, or I should say, messing in the business and the vendors were getting a little uncomfortable that he was sure to pull them down with him. So one night one of their team members got to him and roughed him up a bit too much. Sadly he died. The nun, heir to the business, had a friend, commissioned by the father, who knew the history of what was going on. He had been tracking and following everyone involved. She went to the police and told them all about her dad and about the man who got a bit too rough. She also wanted to make sure all the charges were dropped from the anchorwoman who they were just holding as a sort of bait to tease out the real killer. They ended up cutting a deal and agreed to keep the case out of the papers and never to reveal the dad's involvement. Oh, by the way, they were grateful for that hefty donation to the police's benevolent charity." Joy paused. "You don't remember that episode?"

"Uh, I really don't. Can you tell me what happens to the anchorwoman?"

"Oh, she gets a big fat book contract. I even remember

the agent who was prepared and waiting to offer her a deal." Joy slid a business card across the table to me. She had taken care of everything.

Nearing closing, the restaurant had emptied and eager wait staff stood in the wings prepared to pull up the chairs and start sweeping just as soon as the last diner left the door. Joy took care of the bill while I called Jon to let him know I was ready. We both sat in silence wondering what was next for us.

"You remember how we learned that the purpose of religious life was to remove all obstacles in order to assure our salvation and to be a witness to life everlasting? Well, I am my father's daughter, Kathy. I'm not always a very good person. I need religious life to keep me honest and to keep me whole. Being a nun is a very selfish act for me, especially since I know that I'm not much of a witness." Tears had never been part of Joy's repertoire, but tonight her tears were front and center. I reached in my purse and handed her a tissue.

"Thank you." She paused. "I also need our friendship, Kath. In these last months, as crazy as they have been, I have had the most certainty that I have ever had, that my life was going in the right direction. Rachel has settled down and Jamal is able to make family a top priority. Trenton is even more sure-footed, and well, I am able to work on being more of a witness." She smiled. I smiled back and reached across the table and grabbed her hand in friendship.

Together, we were ready to move on.

ACKNOWLEDGMENTS

Like most writers, I write as a form of communication. First, to learn about myself through the characters I create, the tension that forms in the plots, and how the stories come to resolution. Thus, publishing my work is very important. It is such a great thrill to get that bound book in your hands or to see the words come across on your e-reader. I am grateful to the many people who help to make that happen.

First, to my husband, Mike, who encourages me to write and write and write, because he knows it makes me happy. To my mom, sisters, and family members who serve as inspiration to the characters, I am particularly grateful for their tireless support. I continue to be grateful to Cindy Shearer for the valuable feedback on my writing and positive encouragement of my ideas for the Sister Nun mysteries.

This book is dedicated to the many women religious who continue to inspire me by fostering dialogue and collaboration in these extremely challenging times in the Catholic

Church. Their lives strongly witness to carrying out the gospel in a contemporary, global society. Although it is not hard for me to imagine someone like Sr. Joy Marie with that kind of personality and grounding effectively living religious life today; please know that the characters of Joyce Tucker and the Nelson family are completely fictional.

All of the fans of *They Still Call Me Sister* who continually asked when the next book was coming out, lifted my spirits and made the writing experience of *The Family That Stays Together* even more pleasurable. Thank you for loving the characters, writing great reviews, and rating the book with more stars than I ever imagined my work would receive. As my readers, you are my stars!

CPSIA information can be obtained at www.ICGtesting.com
Printed in the USA
BVOW03s2112141013

333745BV00004B/6/P

9 780615 773636